Frank Athelstane Swettenham

**Malay Sketches**

Frank Athelstane Swettenham

**Malay Sketches**

ISBN/EAN: 9783337289829

Printed in Europe, USA, Canada, Australia, Japan

Cover: Foto ©Andreas Hilbeck / pixelio.de

More available books at **www.hansebooks.com**

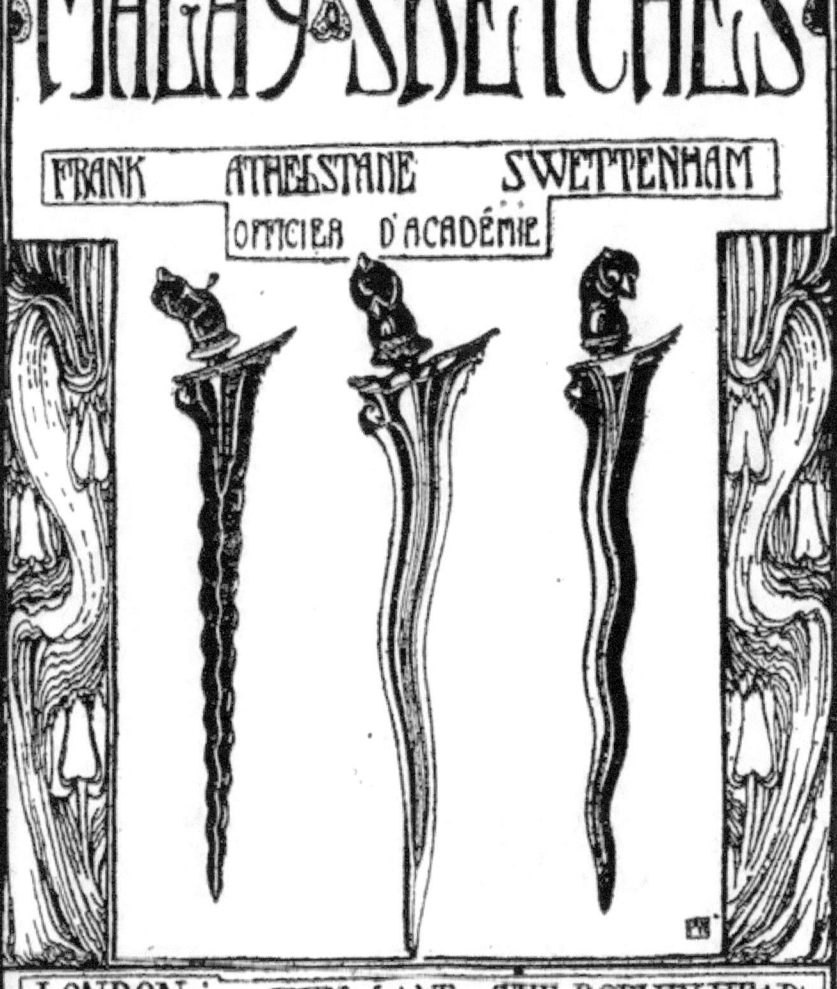

# MALAY SKETCHES

FRANK ATHELSTANE SWETTENHAM
OFFICIER D'ACADÉMIE

LONDON : JOHN LANE · THE BODLEY HEAD ·

NEW YORK · MACMILLAN & CO · MDCCCXCV ·

# CONTENTS

# PREFACE

THIS is not a book of travels, nor is it, in even the smallest sense, the record of a traveller's experiences in a foreign land. It is a series of sketches of Malay scenery and Malay character drawn by one who has spent the best part of his life in the scenes and amongst the people described.

These pages contain no statistics, no history, no geography, no science, real or spurious, no politics, no moralising, no prophecy,—only an attempt to awaken an interest in an almost undescribed but deeply interesting people, the dwellers in one of the most beautiful and least known countries in the East.

The traveller will come in time, and he will publish his experiences of Malâya and the Malays; but while he may look upon the country with a

# PREFACE

higher appreciation and paint its features with a more artistic touch, he will see few of those characteristics of the people, none of that inner life which, I make bold to say, is here faithfully portrayed.

FRANK SWETTENHAM.

THE RESIDENCY,
PERAK, *28 March 1895.*

I MAGINE yourself transported to a land of eternal summer, to that Golden Peninsula, 'twixt Hindustan and Far Cathay, from whence the early navigators brought back such wondrous stories of adventure. A land where Nature is at her best and richest : where plants and animals, beasts of the forest, birds of the air, and every living thing seem yet inspired with a feverish desire for growth and reproduction, as though they were still in the dawn of Creation.

And Man?

Yes, he is here. Forgotten by the world, passed by in the race for civilisation, here he has remained

amongst his own forests, by the banks of his well-
loved streams, unseeking and unsought. Whence
he came none know and few care, but this is the
land that has given to, or taken from, him the name
of a Race that has spread over a wider area than
any other Eastern people.

Malâya, land of the pirate and the *âmok*, your
secrets have been well guarded, but the enemy has
at last passed your gate, and soon the irresistible
Juggernaut of Progress will have penetrated to your
remotest fastness, slain your beasts, cut down your
forests, "civilised" your people, clothed them in
strange garments, and stamped them with the seal
of a higher morality.

That time of regeneration will come rapidly, but
for the moment the Malay of the Peninsula is as he
has been these hundreds of years. Education and
contact with Western people must produce the
inevitable result. Isolated native races whose
numbers are few must disappear or conform to the
views of a stronger will and a higher intelligence.
The Malays of the Peninsula will not disappear,

but they will change, and the process of "awakening" has in places already begun.

It might be rash to speculate on the gain which the future has in store for this people, but it is hardly likely to make them more personally interesting to the observer. This is the moment of transition, and these are sketches of the Malay as he is.

Jetons-nous dans cette petite barque, laissons-nous
aller au courant : une rivière mène toujours à quelque
endroit habité ; si nous ne trouvons pas des choses
agréables, nous trouverons du moins des choses
nouvelles

" ' Allons,' dit Candide, ' recommandons-nous à la
Providence ' "

Voltaire

# MALAY SKETCHES

## I

## THE REAL MALAY

*He was the mildest manner'd man*
*That ever scuttled ship or cut a*
*throat*
BYRON, *Don Juan*

TO begin to understand the Malay you must live in his country, speak his language, respect his faith, be interested in his interests, humour his prejudices, sympathise with and help him in trouble, and share his pleasures and possibly his risks. Only thus can you hope to win his confidence. Only through that confidence can you hope to understand the inner man, and this knowledge can therefore only come to those who have the opportunity and use it.

So far the means of studying Malays in their own country (where alone they are seen in their true character) have fallen to few Europeans, and a very small proportion of them have shown an inclination to get to the hearts of the people. There are a hundred thousand Malays in Perak and some more in other parts of the Peninsula ; and the white man, whose interest in the race is strong enough, may not only win confidence but the devotion that is ready to give life itself in the cause of friendship. The Scripture says : "There is no greater thing than this," and in the end of the nineteenth century that is a form of friendship all too rare. Fortunately this is a thing you cannot buy, but to gain it is worth some effort.

The real Malay is a short, thick-set, well-built man, with straight black hair, a dark brown complexion, thick nose and lips, and bright intelligent eyes. His disposition is generally kindly, his manners are polite and easy. Never cringing, he is reserved with strangers and suspicious, though he does not show it. He is courageous and trustworthy in the discharge of an undertaking ; but he is extravagant, fond of borrowing money, and very slow in repaying it. He is a good talker, speaks in parables, quotes proverbs and wise saws, has a strong sense of humour, and is very fond of a good joke. He takes an interest in the affairs of his neighbours and is consequently a gossip. He is a Muhammadan and a fatalist, but he is also very superstitious. He never drinks intoxicants, he is rarely an opium-smoker. But he is fond of gambling, cock-fighting, and kindred sports. He is by nature a sportsman, catches and tames elephants, is a skilful fisherman, and thoroughly at home in a boat. Above all things, he is conservative to a degree, is proud and fond of his country and his people, venerates his ancient customs and traditions, fears his Rajas, and has a proper respect for constituted authority—while he looks askance on all innovations, and will resist their sudden introduction. But if he has time to examine them carefully, and they are not thrust upon him, he is willing to be convinced of their advantage. At the same time he is a good imitative learner, and, when he has energy and ambition enough for the task, makes a good mechanic. He is, however, lazy to a degree, is without method or order of any kind, knows no regularity even in the hours of his meals, and considers time as of no importance. His house is untidy, even dirty, but he bathes twice a day, and is very fond of personal adornment in the shape of smart clothes.

A Malay is intolerant of insult or slight ; it is something that to him should be wiped out in blood. He will brood over a real or fancied stain on his honour until he is possessed by the desire for revenge. If he cannot wreak it on the offender, he will strike out at the first human being that comes in his way, male or female, old or young. It is this state of blind fury, this vision of blood, that produces the *âmok*. The Malay has often been called treacherous. I question whether he deserves the reproach more than other men. He is courteous and expects courtesy in return, and he understands only one method of avenging personal insults.

The spirit of the clan is also strong in him. He acknowledges the necessity of carrying out, even blindly, the orders of his hereditary chief, while he will protect his own relatives at all costs and make their quarrel his own.

The giving of gifts by Raja to subject, or subject to ruler, is a custom now falling into desuetude, but it still prevails on the occasion of the accession of a Raja, the appointment of high officers, a marriage, a circumcision, ear-piercing, or similar ceremony. As with other Eastern people, hospitality is to the Malay a sacred duty fulfilled by high and low, rich and poor alike.

Though the Malay is an Islam by profession, and would suffer crucifixion sooner than deny his faith, he is not a bigot; indeed, his tolerance compares favourably with that of the professing Christian, and, when he thinks of these matters at all, he believes that the absence of hypocrisy is the beginning of religion. He has a sublime faith in God, the immortality of the soul, a heaven of ecstatic earthly delights, and a hell of punishments, which every individual is so confident will not be his own portion that the idea of its existence presents no terrors.

Christian missionaries of all denominations have apparently abandoned the hope of his conversion.

In his youth, the Malay boy is often beautiful, a thing of wonderful eyes, eyelashes, and eyebrows, with a far-away expression of sadness and solemnity, as though he had left some better place for a compulsory exile on earth.

Those eyes, which are extraordinarily large and clear, seem filled with a pained wonder at all they see here, and they give the impression of a constant effort to open ever wider and wider in search of something they never find. Unlike the child of Japan, this cherub never looks as if his nurse had forgotten to wipe his nose. He is treated with elaborate respect, sleeps when he wishes, and sits up till any hour of the night if he so desires, eats when he is hungry, has no toys, is never whipped, and hardly ever cries.

Until he is fifteen or sixteen, this atmosphere of a better world remains about him. He is often studious even, and duly learns to read the Korân in a language he does not understand.

Then, well then, from sixteen to twenty-five or later he is to be avoided. He takes his pleasure, sows his wild oats like youths of a higher civilisation, is extravagant, open-handed, gambles, gets into debt, runs away with his neighbour's wife, and generally asserts himself. Then follows a period when he either adopts this path and pursues it, or, more commonly, he weans himself gradually from an indulgence that has not altogether realized his expectation, and if, under the advice of older men, he seeks and obtains a position of credit and usefulness in society from which he begins at last to earn some profit, he will, from the age of forty, probably develop into an intelligent man of miserly and rather grasping habits with some one little pet indulgence of no very expensive kind.

The Malay girl-child is not usually so attractive in appearance as the boy, and less consideration is shown to her. She runs wild till the time comes for investing her in a garment, that is to say when

she is about five years old. From then, she is
taught to help in the house and kitchen, to sew, to
read and write, perhaps to work in the *padi* field,
but she is kept out of the way of all strange men-
kind. When fifteen or sixteen, she is often almost
interesting ; very shy, very fond of pretty clothes
and ornaments, not uncommonly much fairer in
complexion than the Malay man, with small hands
and feet, a happy smiling face, good teeth, and
wonderful eyes and eyebrows—the eyes of the little
Malay boy. The Malay girl is proud of a wealth
of straight, black hair, of a spotless olive complexion, of the arch of her brow—" like a one-day-
old moon "—of the curl of her eyelashes, and of the
dimples in cheek or chin.

Unmarried girls are taught to avoid all men
except those nearly related to them. Until marriage, it is considered unmaidenly for them to raise
their eyes or take any part or interest in their
surroundings when men are present. This leads to
an affectation of modesty which, however over-
strained, deceives nobody.

After marriage, a woman gets a considerable
amount of freedom which she naturally values. In
Perak a man, who tries to shut his womenkind up
and prevent their intercourse with others and a

participation in the fêtes and pleasures of Malay society, is looked upon as a jealous, ill-conditioned person.

Malays are extremely particular about questions of rank and birth, especially when it comes to marriage, and *mésalliances*, as understood in the West, are with them very rare.

The general characteristics of Malay women, especially those of gentle birth, are powers of intelligent conversation, quickness in repartee, a strong sense of humour and an instant appreciation of the real meaning of those hidden sayings which are hardly ever absent from their conversation. They are fond of reading such literature as their language offers, and they use uncommon words and expressions, the meanings of which are hardly known to men. For the telling of secrets, they have several modes of speech not understanded of the people.

They are generally amiable in disposition, mildly —sometimes fiercely—jealous, often extravagant and, up to about the age of forty, evince an increasing fondness for jewellery and smart clothes. In these latter days they are developing a pretty taste for horses, carriages, and whatever conduces to luxury and display, though, in their houses, there are still a rugged simplicity and untidiness, absolutely devoid of all sense of order.

A Malay is allowed by law to have as many as four wives, to divorce them, and replace them. If he is well off and can afford so much luxury, he usually takes advantage of the power to marry more than one wife, to divorce and secure successors; but he seldom undertakes the responsibility of four wives at one time. The woman on her part can, and often does, obtain a divorce from her husband. Written conditions of marriage, " settlements " of a kind, are common with people in the upper classes, and the law provides for the custody of children, division of property, and so on. The ancient maiden lady is an unknown quantity, so is the Malay public woman ; and, as there is no society bugbear, the people lead lives that are almost natural. There are no drunken husbands, no hob-nail boots, and no screaming viragoes—because a word would get rid of them. All forms of mad-ness, mania, and brain-softening are extremely rare.

The Malay has ideas on the subject of marriage, ideas born of his infinite experience. He has even soared into regions of matrimonial philosophy, and returned with such crumbs of lore as never fall to the poor monogamist.

I am not going to give away the secrets of the
life behind the curtain ; if I wished to do so I
might trip over difficulties of expression ; but in
spite of the Malay's reputation for bloodthirstiness,
in spite of (or because of, whichever you please) the
fact that he is impregnated with the doctrines of
Islam, in spite of his sensitive honour and his
proneness to revenge, and in spite of his desire to
keep his own women (when young and attractive)
away from the prying eyes of other men, he yet
holds this uncommon faith, that if he has set his
affections on a woman, and for any reason he is
unable at once to make her his own, he cares not
to how many others she allies herself provided she
becomes his before time has robbed her of her
physical attractions.

His reason is this. He says (certainly not to a
stranger, rarely even to his Malay friends, but to
himself) " if, after all this experience, she likes me
best, I have no fear that she will wish to go further
afield. All Malay girls marry before they are
twenty, and the woman who has only known one
husband, however attractive he may be, will come
sooner or later to the conviction that life with
another promises new and delightful experiences
not found in the society of the first man to whom

destiny and her relatives have chosen to unite her.
Thus some fool persuades her that in his worship
and passion she will find the World's Desire, and
it is only after perhaps a long and varied experience
that she realizes that, having started for a voyage
on the ocean, she finds herself seated at the bottom
of a dry well."

It is possible that thus she becomes acquainted
with truth.

# II

# THE TIGER

Yon golden terror, barred with ebon
  stripes
Low-crouching horror, with the cruel
  fangs
Waiting in deathly stillness for thy
  spring
                                    ANON.

SOME idea of what Malays are in their own
  country may best be conveyed by taking the
reader in imagination through some scenes of their
daily life.   The tiger, for instance, is seldom deliberately sought ; if he kills a buffalo a spring gun is
set to shoot him when he returns for his afternoon
meal, but sometimes the tiger comes about a village,
and it is necessary to get rid of so dangerous a
visitor.   Let me try and put the scene before you.

But how describe an Eastern dawn ?   Sight
alone will give a true impression of its strange
beauty.   Out of darkness and stillness, the transi-

tion to light—intense brilliant light—and the sounds
of awakened life, is rapid and complete, a short half
hour or less turning night into tropical day. The
first indication of dawn is a grey haze, then the
clouds clothing the Western hills are shot with pale
yellow and in a few minutes turn to gold, while
Eastern ranges are still in darkness. The light
spreads to the Western slopes, moves rapidly across
the valleys, and suddenly the sun, a great ball of
fire, appears above the Eastern hills. The fogs,
which have risen from the rivers and marshes and
covered the land, as with a pall, rise like smoke and
disappear, and the whole face of nature is flooded
with light, the valleys and slopes of the Eastern
ranges being the last to feel the influence of the
risen sun.

That grey half-light which precedes dawn is the
signal for Malays to be stirring. The doors are
opened, and, only half awake and shivering in the
slight breeze made by the rising fog, they leave
their houses and make for the nearest stream, there
to bathe and fetch fresh water for the day's use.

A woman dressed in the *sârong*, a plaid skirt
of silk or cotton, and a jacket, walks rapidly to the
river, carrying a long bamboo and some gourds,
which, after her bath, she fills, and begins to walk

home through the wealth of vegetation that clothes the whole face of the country. She follows a narrow path up from the bed of the clear stream, the jungle trees and orchards, the long rank grasses and tangled creepers almost hiding the path. Suddenly she stops spellbound, her knees give way under her, the vessels drop from her nerveless hands, and a speechless fear turns her blood to water ; for there, in front of her, is a great black and yellow head with cruel yellow eyes, and a half-open mouth showing a red tongue and long white teeth. The shoulders and fore feet of the tiger stand clear of the thick foliage, and a hoarse low roar of surprise and anger comes from the open mouth. An exceeding great fear chains the terrified woman to the spot, and the tiger, thus faced, sulkily and with more hoarse grumbling, slowly draws back into the jungle and disappears. Then the instinct of self-preservation returns to the woman, and, with knees still weak and a cold hand on her heart, she stumbles, with what speed she may, back to the river, down the bank, and to the friendly shelter of the nearest dwelling.

It takes little time to tell the story, and the men of the house, armed with spears and *krises* and an old rusty gun, quickly spread the news throughout the *kampong*, as each cluster of huts and orchards is called. Every one arms himself with such weapons as he possesses, the boys of sixteen or seventeen climb into trees, from which they hope to see and be able to report the movements of the beast. The men, marshalled by the *ka-tua kampong*, the village chief, make their plans for surrounding the spot where the tiger was seen, and word is sent by messenger to the nearest police-station and European officer.

Whilst all this is taking place, the tiger, probably conscious that too many people are about, leaves his lair and stealthily creeps along a path which will lead him far from habitations. But, as he does so, he passes under a tree where sits one of the young watchmen, and the boy, seizing his opportunity, drops a heavy spear on the tiger as he passes, and gives him a serious wound. The beast, with a roar of pain, leaps into the jungle, carrying the spear with him ; and, after what he considers a safe interval, the boy climbs down, gets back to the circle of watchers, and reports what has occurred.

For a long time, there is silence, no one caring to go in and seek a wounded tiger—but this monotony is broken rudely and suddenly by a shot on the out-skirts of the wide surrounding ring of beaters where a young Malay has been keeping guard over a jungle track. Instantly the nearest rush to the spot only to find the boy badly wounded, after firing a shot that struck the tiger but did not prevent him reaching and pulling down the youth who fired it.

Hardly has a party carried the wounded man to shelter, than news arrives that, in trying to break the ring at another point, the tiger has sprung upon the point of a spear held in rest by a kneeling Malay, and, the spear, passing completely through the beast's body, the tiger has come down on the man's back and killed him. The old men say it is because, regardless of the wisdom of their ancestors, fools now face a tiger with spears unguarded, whereas in the olden time it was always the custom to tie a crosspiece of wood where blade joins shaft to prevent the tiger "running up the spear" and killing his opponent.

The game is getting serious now and the tiger has retired to growl and roar in a thick isolated copse of bushes and tangled undergrowth from which it seems impossible to draw him, and where it would be madness to seek him.

By this time, all the principal people in the neighbourhood have been collected. The copse is sur-

rounded and two elephants are ridden at the cover,
in the hope of driving the wounded tiger from his
shelter. A vain hope, for, when the huge beasts
get inconveniently near to him, the tiger, with a
great roar, springs on to the shoulder of the nearest
elephant and brings him to his knees. The terrified
occupants of the howdah are thus deposited on the
ground, but lose no time in picking themselves up
and getting away. The elephant with a scream of
terror whirls round, throwing off the tiger with a
broken tooth, and, accompanied by his fellow,
rushes from the place and will not be stopped till
several miles have been covered and the river is
between them and their enemy.

Severe maladies want desperate and heroic
remedies. After a short consultation, a young
Malay chief and several of his friends, armed only
with spears, express their determination to seek the
tiger where he lies. They immediately put the plan
into execution. Shoulder to shoulder and with
spears in rest, they advance to the copse. They
have not long to wait in doubt for the wounded and
enraged beast, with open mouth and eyes blazing
fell purpose, charges straight at them. There is the
shock of flesh against steel, an awful snarling and
straining of muscles and the already badly wounded

tiger is pinned to the ground and dies under the thrusts of many spears.

The general result of a tiger hunt, under such circumstances, is the death or serious injury of one or two of the pursuers.

# III

# A FISHING PICNIC

I have given you lands to hunt in,
I have given you streams to fish in,
Filled the river full of fishes
LONGFELLOW

NOW come to a Malay picnic.
Again, it is early morning, the guests have been invited overnight and warned to come on their elephants and bring " rice and salt." By the time the sun is well up there are fifty or sixty people (of whom about half are women), mounted on twelve or fifteen elephants, and some boys and followers are prepared to walk.

The word is given to make for a great limestone hill rising abruptly out of the plain, for, close round the foot of this rock, eating its way into the unexplored depths of subaqueous caves, flows a clear mountain-bred stream, and, in the silent pools which lie under the shadow of the cliff, are the fish which with the rice and salt, will make the coming feast.

The road lies through six or seven miles of open country and virgin forest, and it is 9 or 10 A.M. before the river is reached, the elephants hobbled, and the men of the party ready for business.

In days gone by, the method would have been to *tuba* the stream above a pool, but this poisoning of the water affects the river for miles, and dynamite which is not nearly so destructive is preferred. The plan is to select a large and deep pool round which the men stand ready to spring in, while the women make a cordon across the shallow at its lower end, ready to catch the fish that escape the hands of the swimmers. Two cartridges of dynamite with a detonator and a piece of slow match are tied to a stone and thrown into the deepest part of the pool, there is an explosion sending up a great column of water, and immediately the dead fish come to the surface and begin to float down stream. Twenty men spring into the pool, and with shouts and laughter struggle for the slippery fish ; those which elude the grasp of the swimmers are caught by the women. It will then be probably discovered that no very big fish have been taken ; and, as it is certain that some at least should be there, the boldest and best divers will search the bottom of the pool and even look into the water-filled caves of the rock that there rises sheer out of the stream. Success rewards this effort, and, from the bed of the pool, some sixteen or eighteen feet deep, the divers bring up two at a time, great silvery fish weighing ten to fifteen pounds each. There is much joy over the capture of these *klah* and *tengas*, the best kinds of fresh water fish known here, and, if the total take is not a large one, the operation will be repeated in another and yet another pool, until a sufficient quantity of fish has been secured and every one is tired of the water.

There is a general change of wet garments for dry ones, no difficult matter, while long before this fires have been made on the bank, rice is boiling, fish are roasting in split sticks, grilling, frying, and the hungry company is settling itself in groups ready for the meal. It is a matter of honour that no plates should be used, so every one has a piece of fresh green plantain leaf to hold his rice and salt and fish, while nature supplies the forks and spoons. Whether it is the exercise, the excitement, or the coldness of the two hours' bath, that is most responsible for the keen appetites is not worth inquiring, but thorough justice is done to the food ; and if you, reader, should ever be fortunate enough to take part in one of these picnics, you will declare that you never before realised how delicious a meal can be made of such simple ingredients. Some one has smuggled in a few condiments and they add largely to the success of the Malay *bouille-abaisse*, but people affect not to know they are there, and you go away assured that rice and salt did it all. That is part of the game.

And now it is time to return, the sun has long passed the meridian, and there is a mile or two of forest before getting into the open country. The timid amongst the ladies feign alarm (Malays are sensible people who take only the young to picnics, and leave the old to mind the houses), and a desire to get away at once, but there are others who know what is in store for them.

The elephants are brought up and each pannier is found to be loaded with jungle fruit, large and small, ripe and unripe, hard and soft, but generally hard as stones. Every one knows the meaning of this and, as the elephants kneel down to take their riders, you may observe that usually two men sit in front, two women behind, and the latter are anxious about their umbrellas and show a tendency to open

22

them here where, in the gloom of the forest, they
are not needed. The first two or three elephants
move off quickly, and, having turned a corner in the
path, disappear. It is necessary to proceed in Indian
file, and as the next elephant comes to this corner
he and his company are assailed by a perfect shower
of missiles (the jungle fruit) from the riders of the
first section of elephants who are slily waiting here
to surprise those behind. The attack is returned
with interest and the battle wages hot and furious.
The leaders of the rear column try to force their
way past those who dispute the path with them, and
either succeed or put the enemy to flight only to find
a succession of ambuscades laid for them, each
resulting in a deadly struggle, and so, throughout
the length of the forest, the more venturesome
pushing their way to the front or taking up an
independent line and making enemies of all comers,
until, at last, the whole party clears the jungle and,
taking open order, a succession of wild charges soon
gets every one into the fray and, the supply of ammunition having run out, there is nothing left but to
count the damage done.

It is principally in broken umbrellas which have
been used as shields, but some garments are stained,
and there may be a few bruises treated with much

good humour, and, by the time the party has straightened its dishevelledness, it is found that miles of otherwise tedious journey have been passed and every one is home ere the lengthening shadows suddenly contract and tell the sun has set.

# IV

# THE MURDER OF THE HAWKER

It is a damned and bloody work,
The graceless action of a heavy hand
*King John*

ONE afternoon, in 1892, a foreign Malay named Lenggang, who made a living by hawking in a boat on the Perak River, left Bota with his usual cargo and a hundred dollars which his cousin, the son of the *Penghulu*, had been keeping for him. He was alone in the boat and dropped down stream, saying he would call at some of the villages that line at intervals the banks of the river.

The next day this man's dead body, lying partly under a mosquito curtain, was discovered in the boat as it drifted past the village of Pulau Tiga. The local headman viewed it, but saw nothing to arouse his suspicions, for the boat was full of valuables and a certain amount of money, while nothing in it seemed to have been disturbed, and

25

there were no marks of violence on the corpse, which was duly buried.

When the matter was reported, inquiries were made but they elicited nothing. Some months after the relatives of the dead man appeared at Teluk Anson, and said they had good reason to believe that he had met with foul play, indeed that he had been murdered at a place called Lambor—a few miles below Bota and above Pulau Tiga. An intelligent Malay sergeant of police proceeded to the spot, arrested a number of people, who denied all knowledge of the affair, and took them to Teluk Anson. Arrived there, these people said they were able to give all the necessary information if that would procure their release, as they had only promised to keep their mouths shut so long as they themselves did not suffer for it.

The details of the story as told in evidence are as follows, and they are very characteristic of the Malay :

It appears that the hawker duly arrived in his boat at Lambor, and there tied up for the night to a stake, about twenty feet from the bank of the river. Shortly afterwards a Malay named Ngah Prang, stopped three of his acquaintances walking on the bank, asked them if they had seen the hawker's boat, and suggested that it would be a good thing to rob him. They said they were afraid, and some other men coming up asked one of those to whom the proposal had been made what they were talking about, and, being told, advised him to have nothing to do with the business and the party dispersed.

That evening, at 8 P.M., several people heard cries of " help, help, I am being killed," from the river, and five or six men ran out of their houses down to the bank, a distance of only fifty yards, whence they saw, in the brilliant moonlight, Ngah Prang and two other men in the hawker's boat, the hawker lying flat on his back while one man had both hands at his throat, another held his wrists, and the third his feet ; but it is said that those on the bank heard a noise of rapping as though feet were kicking or hands beating quickly the deck of the boat. It only lasted for a moment and then there was silence.

As those who had been roused by the cries came down the bank they called to the men in the boat, barely twenty feet away, and lighted at their work by the brilliancy of an Eastern moon, to know what they were doing ; they even addressed them by their names, but these gave no answer, and, getting up from off the hawker, untied the boat, one taking a pole and another the rudder and disappeared down the river. The hawker did not move. He was dead.

The witnesses of this tragedy appear then to have returned to their homes and slept peacefully. Several of them naïvely remarked that they heard the next day that the hawker had been found dead in his boat, and it appears that when one of these witnesses, on the following day, met one of the murderers, he asked him what he was doing in Lenggang's boat, and the man replied that they were robbing him, that he held the hawker by the throat, the others by the hands and feet, but that really they had got very little for their trouble.

Meanwhile the three murderers told several of the eye-witnesses of the affair that, if they said anything, it would be the worse for them, and nothing particular occurred till a notice was posted in the Mosque calling upon any one who knew anything about Lenggang's death to report it to the village Headman. Then Ngah Prang, who apparently was the original instigator of the job, as so often happens, thought he would save himself at the expense of his friends, and actually went himself to make a report, and, meeting on the way one of the

eye-witnesses going on a similar errand, he persuaded him to give a qualified promise to help in
denying Ngah Prang's complicity while convicting
the others.

Needless to say that, from the moment the first
disclosure was made and communicated to the
police, resulting in the arrest of a number of those
who had actually witnessed the crime, every smallest
detail was gradually brought to light, the hawker's
property, even his own clothes, gradually recovered,
the money stolen from him traced, and no single
link left wanting in the chain of evidence strong
enough to convict and hang the guilty men. That
indeed was the result.

I have told the story of this crime, which is
devoid of sensational incident, because it will give
some idea of the state of feeling in a real Malay
*kampong* of poor labouring people far from any
outside influence. The man murdered was a Malay ;
the idea that he was worth something which could
be obtained by the insignificant sacrifice of his life
seems to have at once suggested that Providence
was putting a good thing in the way of poor people,
and those who were not afraid determined that the
opportunity was not to be lost. The murder is
discussed practically in public ; it is executed also

in public, in the presence of a feebly expostulating opposition, and then every one goes to bed. The only further concern of the community in the matter is as to how much the murderers got. For them the incident ends there, and, if any one has any qualms of conscience, they are silenced by the threats of the men who so easily throttled the hawker.

It is only when inquiries are pushed, and things are made generally unpleasant for every one, that the truth is unwillingly disclosed, and the penalty paid.

# V

## MĔNG-GĔLUNCHOR

> And falling and crawling and sprawl-
> ing,
> And driving and riving and striving,
> And sprinkling and twinkling and
> winkling,
> And sounding and bounding and
> rounding,
> Dividing and gliding and sliding,
> And trumping and plumping and
> bumping and jumping,
> And dashing and flashing and splash-
> ing and clashing
>
> SOUTHEY

THE Malays of Pêrak occasionally indulge themselves in a form of amusement which, I believe,
is peculiar to them. Though of ancient origin, it is
not well known even here, and, as new sensations
are the desire of our time, I offer it to the iaded
pleasure-seekers of the West.

Given a fine sunny morning (and that is what
most mornings are in Pêrak) you will drive four or

five miles to the appointed place of meeting, and there find a crowd of one or two hundred Malay men, women, and children, who have been duly bidden to *měng-gělunchor* and to take part in the picnic which forms a recognised accompaniment to the proceedings.

A walk of a couple of miles along a shady jungle path brings the party to the foot of a spur of hills, whence a clear mountain stream leaps down a succession of cascades to fertilise the plain. There is a stiff climb for several hundred feet until the party gains a great granite rock in the bed of the stream, large enough to accommodate a much more numerous gathering. In a " spate " this rock might be covered, but now the water flows round it and dashes itself wildly over the falls below. Upstream, however, there is a sheer smooth face of granite, about sixty feet long, inclined at an angle of say 45°, and, while the main body of water finds its way down one side of this rock and then across its foot, a certain quantity, only an inch or two deep, flows steadily down the face. The depth of water here can be increased at will by bamboo troughs, leading out of the great pool which lies at the head of the waterfall. At the base of the rock is an inviting lynn not more than four feet deep. On either

side, the river is shut in by a wealth of jungle
foliage through which the sun strikes at rare
intervals, just sufficiently to give the sense of
warmth and colour.

It is delightfully picturesque with all these people
in their many-coloured garments, grouped in artistic
confusion, on bank and rock. They only sit for a
brief rest after the climb, to collect wood, make fires
and get the work of cooking started, and you will
not be left long in doubt as to the meaning of
*mĕng-gĕlunchor*. It is to slide, and the game is to
"toboggan" down this waterfall into the lynn at its
base.

A crowd of little boys is already walking up the
steep, slippery rock. They go to the very top, sit
down in the shallow water with feet straight out in
front of them and a hand on either side for guidance,
and immediately begin to slide down the sixty feet
of height, gaining, before they have gone half way,
so great a speed that the final descent into the pool
is like the fall of a stone. They succeed each other
in a constant stream, those behind coming on the
top of those who have already reached the lynn.

But now the men, and lastly the women, are drawn
to join the sliders and the fun becomes indeed both
fast and furious. The women begin timidly, only

33                                    c

half way up the slide, but soon grow bolder, and mixed parties of four, six, and eight in rows of two, three, or four each, start together and, with a good deal of laughter and ill-directed attempts at mutual assistance, dash wildly into the pool which is almost constantly full of a struggling, screaming crowd of young people of both sexes.

If you understand the game, the slide is a graceful progress, but, if you don't, if you fail to sit erect, if you do not keep your feet together, above all, if you lose your balance and do not remain absolutely straight on the slide, then your descent will be far from graceful, it may even be slightly painful, and the final plunge into the lynn will be distinctly undignified. It is well to leave your dignity at home, if you go to *měng-gělunchor* with a Malay party, for those who do not weary themselves with tobogganing become absolutely exhausted with laughing at the sliders. The fascination of the thing is extraordinary, and, to read this poor description, you would think it impossible that any sane person would spend hours in struggling up a steep and slippery rock to slide down it on two inches of water, and, having gained a startling velocity, leap into a shallow pool where half a dozen people will be on you before you can get out of the way. And yet I am persuaded that, if your joints are not stiff with age and you are not afraid of cold water, or ridicule, or personal damage (and you will admit none of those things) you would *mĕng-gĕlunchor* with the best of them, nor be the first to cry " hold, enough."

It is usual for the men, when sliding down the rock, to sit upon a piece of the thick fibre of the plantain called *upih*. It is perhaps advisable, but the women do not seem to want it. It is surprising that there are so few casualties and of such small importance—some slight abrasions, a little bumping of heads, at most the loss of a tooth, will be the extent of the total damage, and with a little care there need be none at all.

By 1 P.M. every one will probably be tired, dry garments are donned, and a very hungry company does ample justice to the meal. An hour will be spent in smoking and gossip, and, as the shadows begin to lengthen, a long procession slowly wends its way back, down the slippery descent, across the sunny fields, and through the forest, to the trysting-place where all met in the morning and whence they now return to their own homes.

The intelligent reader will realise that this is a game abounding in possibilities, but the players should be chosen with discrimination and with due regard to individual affinities.

A sunny climate and surroundings of natural beauty are necessary ; but a wooded ravine on the Riviera or by the shore of an Italian lake, a clear stream leaping down a steep rocky bed, and the rest can be easily arranged by a little cutting and polishing of stone.

Besides the novelty and charm of the exercise, the exhilarating motion, the semblance of danger, the clutchings at the nearest straws for help—there are infinite opportunities for designing and donning attractive garments wherein the graceful lines of the human form would be less jealously hidden than in the trappings of stern convention.

Puffed sleeves and a bell skirt, Louis XIV. heels and an eighteen inch waist, would be inconvenient and out of place when sliding down a waterfall in the hope of a safe and graceful plunge into a shallow lynn.

But if the company be well chosen, the *venue* and the climate such as can be found at a hundred places between St. Tropez and Salerno, if there is in the costumes and the luncheon only a fair application of Art to Nature, the Eastern pastime is capable of easy and successful acclimatisation in the West. And as the knights and dames stroll slowly down the wooded glen, and the sinking sun strikes long shafts of light across their path, glorifying all colours, not least the tint of hair and eyes, the pleasure-seekers, if they have not by then found some more mutually interesting topic, will be very unanimous in their praise of *Mĕng-gĕlunchor*.

# VI

# ÂMOK

There comes a time
When the insatiate brute within the
man,
Weary with wallowing in the mire,
leaps forth
Devouring . . . . and the soul sinks
And leaves the man a devil

LEWIS MORRIS

MENTION has been made of the Malay *âmok*, and, as what, with our happy faculty for mispronunciation and misspelling of the words of other languages, is called "running amuck," is with many English people their only idea of the Malay, and that a very vague one, it may be of interest to briefly describe this form of homicidal mania.

*Mèng-âmok* is to make a sudden, murderous attack, and though it is applied to the onslaught of a body of men in war time, or where plunder is the object and murder the means to arrive at it, the term is more commonly used to describe the action of an individual who, suddenly and without apparent cause, seizes a weapon and strikes out blindly, killing and wounding all who come in his way, regardless of age or sex, whether they be friends, strangers, or his own nearest relatives.

Just before sunset on the evening of the 11th February, 1891, a Malay named Imam Mamat (that is Mamat the priest) came quietly into the house of his brother-in-law at Pasir Gâram on the Perak River, carrying a spear and a *gôlok*, *i.e.* a sharp, pointed cutting knife.

The Imam went up to his brother-in-law, took his hand and asked his pardon. He then approached his own wife and similarly asked her pardon, immediately stabbing her fatally in the abdomen with the *gôlok*. She fell, and her brother, rushing to assist her, received a mortal wound in the heart. The brother-in-law's wife was in the house with four children, and they managed to get out before the Imam had time to do more than stab the last of them, a boy, in the back as he left the door. At this moment, a man, who had heard the screams of the women, attempted to enter the house, when the Imam rushed at him and inflicted a slight wound, the man falling to the ground and getting away.

Having secured two more spears which he found in the house, the murderer now gave chase to the woman and her three little children and made short work of them. A tiny girl of four years old and a boy of seven were killed, while the third child received two wounds in the back ; a spear thrust disposed of the mother—all this within one hundred yards of the house.

The Imam now walked down the river bank, where he was met by a friend named Uda Majid, rash enough to think his unarmed influence would prevail over the other's madness.

He greeted the Imam respectfully, and said, "You recognise me, don't let there be any trouble."

The Imam replied, " Yes, I know you, but my spear does not," and immediately stabbed him twice.

Though terribly injured, Uda Majid wrested the spear from the Imam, who again stabbed him twice, this time in lung and windpipe, and he fell. Another man coming up ran unarmed to the assistance of Uda Majid, when the murderer turned on the new-comer and pursued him ; but, seeing Uda Majid get up and attempt to stagger away, the Imam went back to him and, with two more stabs in the back, killed him. Out of the six wounds inflicted on this man three would have proved fatal.

The murderer now rushed along the river bank, and was twice seen to wade far out into the water and return. Then he was lost sight of.

By this time the news had spread up stream and down, and every one was aware that there was abroad an armed man who would neither give nor receive quarter.

For two days, a body of not less than two hundred armed men under the village chiefs made ceaseless but unavailing search for the murderer. At 6 P.M. on the second day, Imam Mamat suddenly appeared in front of the house of a man called Lasam, who had barely time to slam the door in his face and fasten it. The house at that moment contained four men, five women, and seven children, and the only weapon they possessed was one spear.

Lasam asked the Imam what he wanted, and he said he wished to be allowed to sleep in the house. He was told he could do so if he would throw away his arms, and to this the Imam replied by an attempt to spear Lasam through the window. The latter, however, seized the weapon, and with the help of his son, wrested it out of the Imam's hands, Lasam receiving a stab in the face from the *gôlok*. During this struggle, the Imam had forced himself halfway through the window, and Lasam seizing his own spear, thrust it into the thigh of the murderer, who fell to the ground. In the fall, the shaft of the spear broke off, leaving the blade in the wound.

It was now pitch dark, and, as the people of the house did not know the extent of the Imam's injury or what he was doing, a man went out by the back to spread the news and call the village headman. On his arrival the light of a torch showed the Imam lying on the ground with his weapons out of reach, and the headman promptly pounced upon him and secured him.

The Imam was duly handed over to the police and conveyed to Teluk Anson, but he died from loss of blood within twenty-four hours of receiving his wound.

Here is the official list of killed and wounded—

### KILLED.

| | | |
|---|---|---|
| Alang Rasak, wife of Imam Mamat | *aged* | 33 |
| Bilal Abu, brother-in-law of Mamat | ,, | 35 |
| Ngah Intan, wife of Bilal Abu | ,, | 32 |
| Puteh, daughter of Bilal Abu | ,, | 4 |
| Mumin, son of Bilal Abu | ,, | 7 |
| Uda Majid | ,, | 35 |

### WOUNDED.

| | | |
|---|---|---|
| Kasim, son of Bilal Abu | *aged* | 14 |
| Teh, daughter of Bilal Abu | ,, | 6 |
| Mat Sah | ,, | 45 |
| Lasam | | — |

It is terrible to have to add that both the women were far advanced in pregnancy.

Imam Mamat was a man of over forty years of age, of good repute with his neighbours, and I never heard any cause suggested why this quiet, elderly man of devotional habits should suddenly, without apparent reason, develop the most inhuman instincts and brutally murder a number of men, women, and children, his nearest relatives and friends. It is, however, quite possible that the man was suffering under the burden of some real or fancied wrong which, after long brooding, darkened his eyes and possessed him with this insane desire to kill.

An autopsy was performed on the murderer's body, and the published report of the surgeon says: " I hereby certify that I this day made a *post-mortem* examination of the body of Imam Mahomed, and find him to have died from hæmorrhage from a wound on the outer side of right thigh ; the internal organs were healthy except that the membranes of the right side of brain were more adherent than usual."

# VII

# THE JÔGET

Every footstep fell as lightly
As a sunbeam on the river
LONGFELLOW's *Spanish Student*

MALAYS are not dancers, but they pay professional performers to dance for their amusement, and consider that " the better part " is with those who watch, at their ease, the exertions of a small class whose members are not held in the highest respect. The spectacle usually provided is strangely wanting in attraction ; a couple of women shuffling their feet, and swaying their hands in gestures that are practically devoid of grace or even variety—that is the Malay dance—and it is accompanied by the beating of native drums, the striking together of two short sticks held in either hand, and the occasional boom of a metal gong. The entertainment has an undoubted fascination for Malays, but it generally forms part of a theatrical perform-

ance, and for Western spectators it is immeasur-
ably dull.

In one of the Malay States, however, Păhang, it
has for years been the custom for the ruler and one
or two of his near relatives to keep trained dancing
girls, who perform what is called the " Jôget "—a
real dance with an accompaniment of something like
real music, though the orchestral instruments are
very rude indeed.

The dancers, *bûdak jôget*, belong to the Raja's
household, they may even be attached to him by a
closer tie ; they perform seldom, only for the amusement of their lord and his friends, and the public
are not admitted. Years ago I saw such a dance,
and though peculiar to Păhang as far as the Malay
States are concerned, it is probable that it came
originally from Java ; the instruments used by the
orchestra and the airs played are certainly far more
common in Java and Sumatra than in the Peninsula.

I had gone to Păhang on a political mission
acompanied by a friend, and we were vainly
courting sleep in a miserable lodging, when at
I A.M. a message came from the Sultan inviting us
to witness a *jôget*. We accepted with alacrity,
and at once made our way to the *astâna*, a
picturesque, well-built and commodious house on

the right bank of the Păhang river. A palisade enclosed the courtyard, and the front of the house was a very large hall, open on three sides, but covered by a lofty roof of fantastic design supported on pillars. The floor of this hall was approached by three wide steps continued round the three open sides, the fourth being closed by a wooden wall which entirely shut off the private apartments save for one central door over which hung a heavy curtain. The three steps were to provide sitting accommodation according to their rank for those admitted to the *astâna*. The middle of the floor, on the night in question, was covered by a large carpet, chairs were placed for us, and the rest of the guests sat on the steps of the daïs.

When we entered, we saw, seated on the carpet, four girls, two of them about eighteen and two about eleven years old, all attractive according to Malay ideas of beauty, and all gorgeously and picturesquely clothed.

On their heads they each wore a large and curious but very pretty ornament of delicate workmanship—a sort of square flower garden where all the flowers were gold, trembling and glittering with every movement of the wearer. These ornaments were secured to the head by twisted cords of silver and gold.    The girls' hair, combed down in a fringe, was cut in a perfect oval round their foreheads and very becomingly dressed behind.

The bodices of their dresses were made of tight-fitting silk, leaving the neck and arms bare, whilst a white band of fine cambric (about $1\frac{1}{2}$ inches wide), passing round the neck, came down on the front of the bodice in the form of a V, and was there fastened by a golden flower.

Round their waists were belts fastened with large and curiously worked *pinding* or buckles of gold, so large that they reached quite across the waist. The rest of the costume consisted of a skirt of cloth of gold (not at all like the *sârong*), reaching to the ankles, while a scarf of the same material, fastened in its centre to the waist-buckle, hung down to the hem of the skirt.

All four dancers were dressed alike, except that the elder girls wore white silk bodices with a red and gold handkerchief, folded cornerwise, tied under the arms and knotted in front.    The points of the handkerchief hung to the middle of the back.    In the case of the two younger girls the entire dress was of one material.

On their arms the dancers wore numbers of gold bangles, and their fingers were covered with diamond

rings. In their ears were fastened the diamond
buttons so much affected by Malays, and indeed
now by Western ladies. Their feet, of course,
were bare.

We had ample time to minutely observe these
details before the dance commenced, for when we
came into the hall the four girls were sitting down
in the usual* Eastern fashion, on the carpet, bending
forward, their elbows resting on their thighs, and
hiding the sides of their faces, which were towards
the audience, with fans made of crimson and gilt
paper which sparkled in the light.

On our entrance the band struck up, and our
special attention was called to the orchestra, as the
instruments are seldom seen in the Malay Peninsula.

There were two chief performers, one playing on
a sort of harmonicon, the notes of which he struck
with pieces of stick held in each hand. The other,
with similar pieces of wood, played on inverted
metal bowls. Both these performers seemed to
have sufficiently hard work, but they played with
the greatest spirit from 10 P.M. till 5 A.M.

The harmonicon is called by Malays *chĕlempong*,
and the inverted bowls, which give a pleasant and

---

* The attitude is that obtained by transferring the body
directly from a kneeling to a sitting position.

musical sound like the noise of rippling water, a *gambang*. The other members of the orchestra consisted of a very small boy who played, with a very large and thick stick, on a gigantic gong—an old woman who beat a drum with two sticks, and several other boys who played on instruments like triangles called *chânang*.

All these performers, we were told with much solemnity, were artists of the first order, masters and a mistress in their craft, and if vigour of execution counts for excellence they proved the justice of the praise.

The Hall, of considerable size, capable of accommodating several hundreds of people, was only dimly lighted, but the fact that, while the audience was in semi-darkness, the light was concentrated on the performers added to the effect. Besides ourselves I question whether there were more than twenty spectators, but sitting on the top of the daïs near to the dancers it was hard to pierce the surrounding gloom.

The orchestra was placed on the left of the entrance to the Hall, that is rather to the side and rather in the background, a position evidently chosen with due regard to the feelings of the audience.

From the elaborate and vehement execution of

the players, and the want of regular time in the music, I judged, and rightly, that we had entered as the overture began. During its performance, the dancers sat leaning forward, hiding their faces as I have described; but when it concluded and, without any break, the music changed into the regular rhythm for dancing, the four girls dropped their fans, raised their hands in the act of *Sèmbah* or homage, and then began the dance by swaying their bodies and slowly waving their arms and hands in the most graceful movements, making much and effective use all the while of the scarf hanging from their belts.

Gradually raising themselves from a sitting to a kneeling posture, acting in perfect accord in every motion, then rising to their feet, they floated through a series of figures hardly to be exceeded in grace and difficulty, considering that the movements are essentially slow, the arms, hands and body being the real performers whilst the feet are scarcely noticed and for half the time not visible.

They danced five or six dances, each lasting quite half an hour, with materially different figures and time in the music. All these dances I was told were symbolical; one, of agriculture, with the tilling of the soil, the sowing of the seed, the reaping and winnowing of the grain, might easily have been guessed from the dancer's movements. But those of the audience whom I was near enough to question were, Malay-like, unable to give me much information. Attendants stood or sat near the dancers and from time to time, as the girls tossed one thing on the floor, handed them another. Sometimes it was a fan or a mirror they held, sometimes a flower or small vessel, but oftener their hands were empty, as it is in the management of the fingers that the chief art of Malay dancers consists.

The last dance, symbolical of war, was perhaps the best, the music being much faster, almost inspiriting, and the movements of the dancers more free and even abandoned. For the latter half of the dance they each held a wand, to represent a sword, bound with three rings of burnished gold which glittered in the light like precious stones.

This nautch, which began soberly, like the others, grew to a wild revel until the dancers were, or pretended to be, possessed by the Spirit of Dancing, *hantu mènâri* as they called it, and leaving the Hall for a moment to smear their fingers and faces with a fragrant oil, they returned, and the two eldest, striking at each other with their wands seemed inclined to turn the symbolical into a real battle. They were, however, after some trouble, caught by four or five women and carried forcibly out of the Hall, but not until their captors had been made to feel the weight of the magic wands. The two younger girls, who looked as if they too would like to be "possessed," but did not know how to accomplish it, were easily caught and removed.

The band, whose strains had been increasing in wildness and in time, ceased playing on the removal of the dancers, and the nautch, which had begun at 10 P.M., was over.

The Raja, who had only appeared at 4 A.M., told me that one of the elder girls, when she became "properly possessed," lived for months on nothing but flowers, a pretty and poetic conceit.

As we left the Astana, and taking boat rowed slowly to the vessel waiting for us off the river's mouth, the rising sun was driving the fog from the numbers of lovely green islets, that seemed to float like dew-drenched lotus leaves on the surface of the shallow stream.

# VIII

# THE STORY OF MAT ARIS

I smote him as I would a worm.
With heart as steeled, with nerve as
firm;
He never woke again

WHITTIER

I T was in the year 1876 that a man named Mat
Aris, of no occupation and less repute, persuaded one Sâhit to take his wife Salâmah and
start on a journey through the jungle to a distant
country. The interest of Mat Aris in this couple
was a desire to get rid of Sâhit and possess himself
of the woman Salâmah, for whom he had conceived
an overmastering passion.

The travellers began their journey at a spot many
miles up the Perak River; their road lay along a
jungle track, and so sparsely inhabited was the
country they were to pass through, that they could
not even find a habitation in which to pass the
night. They had to look forward to many days'

journey through the primæval forest, the home of wild beasts and Sakai people, aboriginal tribes almost as shy and untamed as the elephant, the bison and the rhinoceros, with which they share the forests of the interior.

Sâhit and his wife started on their journey in the company of two brothers of Mat Aris, but meeting him the brothers returned, Mat Aris undertaking the part of escort. In the afternoon of the first day's march a Sakai named Pah Patin met the three, and, being known to Mat Aris, that worthy ordered him to accompany them. Pah Patin did as he was told, and when evening came on, as there was no dwelling within miles, a shelter was built in the jungle wherein the night was to be passed.

It is as well to understand what a Malay jungle is like, for a good soil, well watered, in one of the hottest and dampest climates in the world, produces a forest that is not altogether the counterpart of all other forests.

The reading public, no doubt, believes that the jungle of Darkest Africa is a place of gloom, terror and difficulty without parallel. It may be so, but few of those who know it have visited Malâya, and one is apt to exaggerate one's own troubles. Whatever gruesome peculiarities there are about the African jungle, it seems possible for large bodies of men and women to make their way through it at a fair pace without great difficulty. In that respect at least it has the advantage of the Malay forest.

To begin with there are the trees of all sizes, from the smallest shoot to the giants of the jungle, towering to a height of 150 feet. I know that is not excessive, but in this forcing climate there are an enormous number of such trees, treading on each others roots and crowding the older and feebler out of existence. These are nothing, they afford a pleasant shade from the pitiless rays of the sun, and though this mitigated light cannot by any stretch of imagination be called darkness, it is possible to take off your hat without fear of sunstroke. If it were only for the trees jungle walking would be pleasant enough.

Under them, however, there is an undergrowth so thick as to beggar description. Every conceivable kind of palm, of bush, of creeper, flourishes there with a luxuriance, with a prodigality of vegetable life, that shows how richly Nature deserves her title of Mother. It is a curious fact, remarked by every one who has been brought in contact with the Malay forest, that a very large number of its shrubs, many of its palms, and most of its creepers are armed with spikes of various length, but all of about equal sharpness. Some are so formidable that the thickest skinned beasts avoid contact with them, and no human apparel has been devised, short of armour, that will resist their powers of penetration and destruction. Under the creepers lie fallen trees, and the ground is covered with ferns, rank grasses, and what is generally termed undergrowth, so thick that the soil is often entirely hidden. It may be added as a minor but unpleasant detail that this tangle of vegetation harbours every species of crawling, jumping, and flying unpleasantness ; myriads of leeches that work their way through stockings and garments of any but the closest texture ; centipedes, scorpions, wasps, and stinging flies, caterpillars that thrust their hairs into the skin and leave them there to cause intolerable irritation, snakes poisonous and otherwise, ants with the most murderous proclivities, and last, but not least, mosquitoes that, when they find a human being, make the most of their opportunity. I have not exhausted the catalogue of pests, but only given a sample of what any traveller will meet in a day's journey through a Malay jungle. There is a wasp called "the reminder," a thorn called " Kite's talons," and an ant known as the " fire ant." The names are as apt as they are suggestive.

To force a way through such a place is an impossibility, even on all fours it could not be crawled through, the only means of progress is by cutting a path.

No one attempts to walk through virgin forest unless he be in pursuit of game, or has some special object and the means to clear his way. All Malay jungle is not as thick as that I have described, and as the beasts sought by the sportsman naturally frequent the more open places, tracking is possible, though severe enough work even at the slow rate of progress necessary to enable the pursuers to approach the quarry without being seen or heard.

The lower and more swampy the country the thicker the undergrowth, and I have often noticed that, where a river flows between low banks clothed with virgin forest, it would be almost impossible for even a strong swimmer to force his way out of the water on to the land through the thickly interlaced tangle of branches, rattans, and other thorny creepers that stretch their uninviting arms from the bank far over the water of the stream.

It will naturally be asked how travellers make their way through jungle such as I have described. The reply is that there are existing tracks (not worthy of the name of footpaths) which have been used for ages, originally no doubt formed by the passing and repassing of wild beasts, then adopted by the Sakais, and lastly by Malays. In other cases similar means of passage have been formed by driving tame elephants through the forest from place to place. For the pedestrian, especially if he be clad in the garments and boots of western civilisation, progress through the succession of holes filled with water and mud which marks the track of elephants is neither rapid nor pleasant.

That is the jungle of daylight.

When once the sun has set darkness falls upon everything within the forest, and it is a darkness so absolute as to give to wide-open eyes the impression of blindness. Those who have been so unfortunate as to be benighted in a Malay jungle without torches or lanterns know that there is nothing to be done but to sit down and wait for day.

Such were the surroundings in which Sâhit and his wife found themselves compelled to spend a night in the company of Mat Aris and his Sakai acquaintance.

Mat Aris had a house in this neighbourhood, and on the day following the events already narrated a Malay went to the Headman of his village and said there was a woman in the house of Mat Aris sobbing and saying her husband had been murdered. The Headman went to the place and saw Mat Aris was there and a woman with him. Mat Aris had a reputation which probably induced this Headman not to attempt to interfere with him further than to keep a watch on his proceedings.

In places where there are no roads, and often when they do exist, Malays live on or close by the bank of a river, and, on the following day, the Headman observed Mat Aris and the woman in a boat going down the stream, here a succession of rapids and very difficult to navigate. The Headman followed by a jungle track, and getting near to a place called Kota Tampan, the first police station, he hurried on and gave the information he possessed.

When Mat Aris arrived at Kota Tampan he landed, and was at once arrested by the native sergeant in charge of the station, who accused him of murdering Sâhit. Mat Aris denied the charge, but the woman said her name was Salâmah, and the sergeant said he must take them both to his Divisional Headquarters at Kuala Kangsar, distant thirty miles or more by river. Accordingly the sergeant and some police entered the boat and a start was made for Kuala Kangsar. It shortly appeared that the police, who were natives of India, were not very skilful in the management of the boat, and, as Mat Aris offered his services to steer and there was no doubt of his ability, this important post was given to him. Choosing a convenient place where the stream was both deep and rapid, Mat Aris upset the boat and threw every one into the water. Then seizing the woman, he swam with her to the opposite bank and they both disappeared. The police had enough to do, hampered by their uniforms, to get out of the river with their lives.

For the next eight years Mat Aris eluded all attempts at capture. He lived in the jungle beyond the jurisdiction of the Perak Government, and, with his brothers, became the terror of the neighbourhood, levying black mail on all who passed his way. Mat Aris was the ringleader, and even more serious crimes were laid at his door.

The woman Salâmah was known to be living with Mat Aris as his wife, and it was also known that she had a child by him. Of Sâhit nothing more was seen or heard.

Meanwhile the Government of Perak had established a station in the neighbourhood of the spot where Sâhit had disappeared, and complaints of the lawless proceedings of Mat Aris were constantly

made to the officer in charge of it, but he was helpless, for the outlaw was beyond his reach.

Eight years is, however, a long time, especially
to an Eastern, and travellers worth robbing having
grown scarce, Mat Aris, in the consciousness of his
own rectitude, went to the Perak officer and asked
for work. That mistaken step resulted in his arrest
on the strength of the warrant issued eight years
before.

This time the prisoner was conveyed in safety
to Kuala Kangsar, where he was duly tried.

It is one thing to give information against a man
who is free, willing, and able to resent it, and quite
a different thing to say what you know when that
man is in the toils. There was a witness who was
likely to know what had happened to Sâhit, and that
was Pah Patin the Sakai, but Pah Patin did not
speak, and Mat Aris and Salâmah were the only
other people who knew what he could say. At
least that appeared to be so, for who else would be
likely to know what happened at night in the depths
of the jungle miles from the nearest habitation?

As for Salâmah, like the Sabine women, she
seemed to have reconciled herself to her captor.

But the strange part of this story is that, impossible as it may seem, there was a witness who

saw what took place in that hut in the forest, whither the unsuspecting Sâhit had been lured with his wife under the escort of Mat Aris.

That witness was a Sakai man who had been collecting *gètah* (gutta-percha), and, attracted by the firelight, noiselessly approached the hut and, whilst wondering at the unusual sight of these strangers sleeping in his wild and lonely jungle, he saw Mat Aris get up and stab to death the man, who stood between him and the woman he had determined to possess.

The Sakai saw more than that, but when once he had disclosed what he knew, Pah Patin was found and induced to tell his tale, and other Sakais completed the narrative.

It will be remembered that Sâhit and his wife, Mat Aris and the Sakai Pah Patin had built a shelter where they proposed to spend the night. A fire was lighted, food was cooked and eaten, and the four lay down to sleep. On one side of the fire Mat Aris, next him Salâmah, and then Sâhit; on the other was the Sakai.

The man and his wife slept, the other Malay pretended to sleep, and the Sakai fell into that state which passes for sleep with creatures that are always on the alert for possible danger.

Half an hour later Mat Aris rose up softly and with a *kris* stabbed Sâhit in the throat. The wretched man staggered to his feet, fell and tried to struggle up again when Mat Aris shouted to the Sakai to strike him or he would kill him also. Pah Patin obeyed, and hit the wounded man on the head with a stick. " Then," said Pah Patin when at last he told the story, " there was a little life in him, but he never moved after I struck him."

The woman rushed out of the hut, but Mat Aris followed her and brought her back to the mat by the body of the murdered man, and there they slept together, the Sakai returning to his place on the other side of the fire. The night was young then.

Before daylight Pah Patin left Mat Aris and Salâmah still sleeping by the corpse, and by order of Mat Aris fetched two more Sakais, and these three buried Sâhit by the bank of the river in the presence of Mat Aris and the woman.

Years afterwards, when the details were known, an attempt was made to find the body, but it failed ; decomposition in this climate is rapid, even bones disappear, and the river had many times flooded its banks, trees had gone and others grown, the land-marks were no longer the same, and possibly the exact site of the grave was missed.

# IX

# LÂTAH

Ofttimes he falleth into the fire and
oft into the water
MATTHEW xvii. 14

IN the spring of 1892 I was privileged, by the kindness of a friend and the courtesy of Dr. Luys, to visit the Hospital *de la Charité* in Paris, where I witnessed some very remarkable and interesting experiments in suggestion. There were patients undergoing successful treatment for nervous disorders where the disease was in process of gradual relief by passing from the afflicted person to a medium without injury to the latter ; there was the strange power of hypnotising, influencing and awakening certain *sujets* whose nervous organisations seem to be specially susceptible, and there was the astonishing influence of the magnet over these same *sujets* when already hypnotised. There is something more than usually uncanny in the sight of a person filled with an inexplicable and unnatural delight in the contemplation of the positive end of a magnet, and when the negative end is suddenly turned towards him, to see him instantly fall down unconscious as though struck by lightning.

The *sujets* (there were two of them, a man and a woman) described the appearance of the positive end of the magnet as producing a beautiful blue flame about a foot high, so exquisite in colour and beauty that it transported them with delight. As to the negative end, they reluctantly explained, in hesitating words and with every appearance of dread, that there also was a flame, but a red one of fearful and sinister import.

I was deeply interested in these " manifestations," both for their own strangeness and because I had in the Malay Peninsula seen equally extraordinary proceedings of a somewhat similar kind.

Amongst Malays there is a well-known disease (I use the word for want of a better) called *lâtah;* it is far more common at certain places than at others, and amongst certain divisions of the great Malay family. Thus while there is generally one or more *ôrang lâtah* to be found in every *kampong* in Krian, where the Malays are mostly from Kĕdah, in other

parts of Perak it is rare to ever meet a *lâtah* person.
Again, speaking generally, the disease seems to be
more common amongst the people of Amboina, in
Netherlands India, than those of Java, Sumatra or
the Malay Peninsula. In both cases heredity is probably accountable for the result, whatever may have
been the original cause to produce the affliction in
certain places more than in others. I can only
speak of my own experience and what I have
personally seen, for no English authority appears
to have studied the matter or attempted to either
observe *lâtah* people, diagnose the disease (if it is
one), search for its cause or attempt to cure it. I
can vouch for facts but nothing more.

In 1874 I was sent in H.M.S. *Hart* to reside
with the Sultan of Selangor. Though His Highness's personal record was one of which he might
be proud, for he was said to have killed ninety-nine
men (*sa' râtus kûrang sâtu*) with his own hand, his
State was not altogether a happy one, for it had
been the fighting-ground of several ambitious young
Rajas for some years. An unusually hideous piracy,
personally conducted by one of the Sultan's own
sons, and committed on a Malacca trading vessel,
had necessitated a visit from the China fleet, and
when the perpetrators, or those who after due

inquiry appeared to be the perpetrators, had been executed (the Sultan lending his own *kris* for the ceremony), I was sent to see that these "boyish amusements," as His Highness called them, were not repeated. The place where the Sultan then lived was hardly a desirable residence, even from a Malay point of view, and it has for years now been almost deserted. *Bandar Tèrmâsa*, as it was grandiloquently styled, was a collection of huts on a mud flat enclosed between the Langat and Jugra rivers. It was only seven miles from the sea, and at high tide most of the place was under water.

With me there went twenty-five Malay police from Malacca, and we lived all together in an old stockade on the bank of the Langat river. Whether it was the mosquitoes, which for numbers and venom could not be matched, or whether it was the evil reputation of the place for deeds of violence is needless to inquire, but the police were seized with panic and had to be replaced by another batch from Singapore, selected not so much on account of their virtues as their so-called vices. The exchange was satisfactory, for whatever sins they committed they showed no signs of panic.

Later on I was encouraged by the statement that Bandar Tĕrmâsa, for all its unpromising appearance, was a place for *men*, where those who had a difference settled it promptly with the *kris*, and cowards who came there either found their courage or departed. A story that amused the gossips was that, as a badly wounded man was carried from the duelling field past the palisade which enclosed the Sultan's house, His Highness had asked, through the bars, what was the matter, and, being told, had laconically remarked, "If he is wounded, doctor him ; if he is dead, bury him."

During my residence in the place a lady, for jealousy, stabbed a man of considerable note thirteen times with his own dagger, and sent the next morning to know whether I would like to purchase it, as she did not much fancy the weapon. The man was not killed, and made no complaint. Another lady, for a similar reason, visited our stockade one night, pushed the sentry on one side, and, finding the man she wanted, attempted to stab him with a long *kris* she had brought for that purpose.

That was then the state of society in Bandar Tĕrmâsa.

I have said we lived all together in a stockade. It was a very rude structure with log walls about six feet thick and eight feet high, a mud floor, a thatch roof, and no doors. Outside it was a high watch-tower of the same materials, but the ladder to it had fallen down. Of roads there were none, but a mud path ran through the stockade from river bank to village, distant some 300 yards. My own accommodation was a cot borrowed from the *Hart* and slung between two posts, while the men slept on the walls of the stockade.

The place had drawbacks other than mosquitoes, for the public path ran through it, the tide at high water completely covered the floor, and the log walls were full of snakes. The state of the sur-roundings will best be understood when I say that during the many months I lived there I did not wear boots outside the stockade, because there was nothing to walk upon but deep mud, and that the only water fit to use was contained in a well or pond a quarter of a mile off, to which I walked every day to bathe.

With the second batch of police had come an European inspector, and he and I were the only white men in the country.

Amongst the twenty-five police were two men of the name of Kâsim; they were both natives of Amboina, but very different in disposition, and they were known among their comrades as Kâsim *Bĕsar* and Kâsim *Kéchil*—that is Kâsim Major and Kâsim Minor.

Kâsim Major was a quiet, reserved, silent man of about twenty-five, and I afterwards realised that he had a somewhat violent temper when roused. Kâsim Minor, on the contrary, was a smiling, talkative, happy, and pleasant-looking young fellow of about twenty. They were not related to each other in any way.

I used often to be away on the coast and up river, and on my return from one of these expeditions I noticed the men teasing Kâsim Minor, and saw at once that he was *lâtah*. I questioned the inspector, and he told me that during my absence he had one day been away on duty for some hours, and when he returned, about 4 P.M., he saw Kâsim Minor up a coco-nut tree just outside the stockade. On asking him what he was doing there, he replied he could not come down because there was a snake at the bottom of the tree. In reality there was a bit of rattan tied round the tree, and, this being removed, Kâsim came down.

Now, it is no easy matter to climb a coco-nut tree ; it requires a special training to do it at all, and Kâsim did not possess it. But the inspector ascertained that the other police had found out by

accident that their comrade was *lâtah*, that they had
ordered him to climb the tree, which he had at
once done, and that then, out of sheer devilry,
some one had taken a bit of rattan, said, " Do you
see this snake ? I will tie it round the tree, and
then you can't come down," and so left him from
10 A.M. till the afternoon, when the inspector
returned and released him.

The time of Kâsim's penance was probably
greatly exaggerated, but that is how the story was
told to me, and of all that follows I was an eye-
witness.

I made Kâsim Minor my orderly, and as he was
constantly with me I had better opportunities of
studying his peculiarities. About this time also I
learnt that Kâsim Major was also *lâtah*.

Speaking generally, it was only necessary for any
one to attract the attention of either of these men
by the simplest means, holding up a finger, calling
them by name in a rather pointed way, touching
them or even, when close by, to look them hard in
the face, and instantly they appeared to lose all
control of themselves and would do, not only whatever they were told to do, but whatever was suggested by a sign.

I have seen many *lâtah* people, male and female,

but never any quite like these two, none so susceptible to outside influence, so ready to blindly obey a word or a sign.

The kindly disposition of Kâsim Minor made him quite harmless, but the other Kâsim was rather a dangerous subject to play tricks with, as I will presently explain.

The *lâtah* man or woman usually met with, if suddenly startled, by a touch, a noise, or the sight of something unexpected, will not only show all the signs of a very nervous person but almost invariably will fire off a volley of expressions more or less obscene, having no reference at all to the circumstance which has suddenly aroused attention. As a rule it is necessary to *startle* these people before they will say or do anything to show that they are differently constituted to their neighbours, and when they have betrayed themselves either by word or deed their instinct is to get away as quickly as possible. Children and even grown-up people cannot always resist the pleasure of " bating " a *lâtah* person ; for one reason because it is so exceedingly easy, for another because they are inclined on the spur of the moment to do ludicrous things or say something they would under ordinary circumstances be ashamed of. *Almost* invariably *lâtah* people of this class (and it is by far the most common one) are very good humoured and never seem to think of resenting the liberty taken with their infirmity. If by word or deed they commit themselves (and that is not uncommon) they either run away, or appear to be unconscious of having said or done anything unusual (this however is rare), or they simply say, " I am *lâtah*," as a full explanation and excuse.

If any one present accidentally drops something on the floor, if a lizard falls from the roof on to or near a *lâtah* person, if the wind blows the shutter of a window to with a bang, a *lâtah* person of the class I speak of will probably find it necessary to at least say something not usually heard in polite society. Of this class by far the majority are women.

I have never seen a *lâtah* boy or girl, but I know they are to be found, though the disease certainly becomes more evident as the subject grows older.

It must be understood that except when under influence, when actually showing the evidences of this strange peculiarity, *lâtah* people are undistinguishable from others. It is sufficient proof of this that amongst my twenty-five police there should have been two men more completely *lâtah* than any I have seen before or since.

I took occasion to carefully observe the two Kâsims. It was impossible to always prevent their companions teasing them, especially in a place where there was absolutely no form of amusement and all the conditions of life were as unpleasant as they well could be, but no harm was ever done, and I am satisfied that while influence was in any way exercised over the *lâtah* man he was not conscious of his own actions, and directly it was removed he became his reasoning other self, and the utmost that remained on his mind, or came to him with the recovery of his own will, was that he might have done something foolish.

If the attention of either of these men was arrested, as I have said by word, sign, or a meaning glance, from that moment until the influence was removed, the *lâtah* man would do whatever he was told or signed to do without hesitation, whether the act signified were difficult, dangerous, or painful. When once under this influence any one present could give the order and the *lâtah* man would immediately obey it ; not only that, but even at some distance (as in the coco-nut tree incident), he appeared to be equally subject to the will imposed on his actions.

A curious thing about both these men was that,

having attracted the attention of either, if you said, " Kâsim, go and hit that man," he would invariably repeat what was said, word for word, including his own name, while he carried out the order. When the person hit turned on him, Kâsim would say, "It was not I who hit you, but that man who ordered me."

I have seen Kâsim the younger, when the man influencing him put his own finger in his mouth and pretended to bite it, imitate the action but really bite his finger and bite it hard. Similarly I have seen him, in imitation and without a word being said, take a lighted brand from the fire, and he would have put it in his mouth if the experiment had been carried so far. Some one told him one day to jump into the river, and he did not get out again till he had swum nearly two hundred yards, for the stream was both broad and deep, with a terrible current, and infested by crocodiles. If at any moment you called out " Tôlong Kâsim " ("help ! Kâsim "), the instant he heard it he would jump up and crying " Tôlong Kâsim," dash straight to you over all obstacles. If then you had put a weapon in his hand and told him to slay any one within reach I have not the slightest doubt he would have done it without hesitation.

I have said there was a ladderless watch-tower outside the stockade. The police wanted firewood, they were not allowed to burn the logs forming our walls, but at the top of the watch-tower there were also log walls that they were told they could burn. They were lazy, however, and did not see how they were going to get up, so they ordered Kâsim the younger to climb up, which he did as he had climbed the coco-nut tree, and, when once there, they told him to throw down logs until they thought they had enough. I watched that operation, and the feverish haste with which the man swarmed up one of the supports, gained the platform of the tower, and threw down huge logs as though his life depended on it, was rather remarkable. I gave orders that the man's infirmity was not to be used for this purpose again, but in my absence I know that when more firewood was wanted Kâsim went up to the watch-tower for it until that supply was exhausted.

The path from the stockade to the village was in sight of the stockade throughout its length, and one day I noticed Kâsim Minor, as he walked leisurely down this mud embankment, stop every now and then and behave in a peculiar fashion as though he were having conversation with the frogs, snakes and other denizens of the ditches that bordered the path. When he had gone half way he stopped and peeped up into the branches of a small tree on the road side, then he seemed to be striking blows at an invisible enemy, ran to the ditch and began throwing lump after lump of hard mud into the tree. I had not seen this phase of his peculiarities before and could not make it out, but suddenly his arms went about his head like the sails of a windmill, and I realised that his enemies were bees or hornets, and that he was getting a good deal the worst of an unequal fight. I sent some of the men to fetch him back and found he had been rather badly stung, and when I asked him why he attacked the nest he said his attention was caught by things flying out of the tree and he was impelled to throw at them.

I understood that the hornets flying out of the nest appeared to be thrown at him, and he could not help imitating what he saw in the best way he could, and so he took what was nearest his hand and sent it flying back.

Kâsim the elder was quite as susceptible as his namesake, but his comrades were a little shy of provoking him as they soon realised that his temper made the amusement dangerous. One day they must have been teasing him, and, when he was allowed to recover his own will, I suppose their laughter made it evident to him that he had made himself ridiculous, for he suddenly ran to the arm-rack, and seizing a sword bayonet made for his tormentors with such evident intention to use it that they precipitately fled, and in a few seconds were making very, good time across the swamp with Kâsim and the drawn sword far too close to be pleasant. I had some difficulty in persuading him to abandon his purpose, but after that and a lecture his comrades did not greatly bother him.

I remember, however, that on another occasion we had secured and erected a long thin spar to serve as a flagstaff, but the halyard jammed and it seemed necessary to lower the spar when some one called out to Kâsim the elder to climb up it. Before I could interfere, he had gone up two-thirds of the height, and he only came down reluctantly. Had he gone a few feet higher the pole would inevitably have snapped and he would have had a severe fall.

About this time a friend came and shared my loneliness for a fortnight. He had had experience of *lâtah* people before, but the two Kâsims were rather a revelation, and he was perhaps inclined to doubt what I told him they could be made to do.

One morning we were bathing as usual at the pond, and Kâsim the younger was in attendance carrying the towels, &c.

The bath was over, and we were all three standing on the bank, when my friend said to Kâsim :

"*Mâri, kîta tèrjun*" (come, let us jump in), at the same time feigning to jump. Kâsim instantly jumped into the pond, disappeared, came up spluttering, and having scrambled out, said : "*Itu tîdak baik, Tûan*" (that is not good of you, sir).

My friend said, " Why, I did nothing, I only said let us jump in and went like this," repeating his previous action, when Kâsim immediately repeated his plunge, and we dragged him from the water looking like a retriever.

When I was first ordered to Selangor, I thought it possible that some sort of furniture might be useful, and I took up a few chairs and other things, including a large roll of what is known as Calcutta matting. The things were useless in a place where the mud floor was often under water twice during twenty-four hours, and they lay piled in a corner of the stockade, and whenever a Malay of distinction came to see me for whom it was necessary to find a chair, it was advisable to see that the seat was not already occupied by a snake. The roll of matting, about four feet high and two-and-a-half feet in diameter naturally remained unopened.

Every night, owing to the myriads of mosquitoes, a large bonfire was lit in the middle of the stockade, for only in the smoke of that fire was it possible to eat one's dinner. One night some Malays from the village had come in, and the police were trying to amuse them and forget their own miseries by dancing and singing round the fire. Under such circumstances Malays have a happy knack of making the best of things, they laugh easily and often, and as I have said elsewhere, they have a strong sense of humour if not always of a very refined description. Some one had introduced one of the Kâsims, in his character of an *órang lâtah*, for the benefit of the strangers, and one of the men was inspired to fetch the roll of matting, and solemnly presenting it to Kâsim the younger, said, "Kâsim, here is your wife."

Even now I do not forget the smile of beatitude and satisfaction with which Kâsim Minor regarded that undesirable and figureless bundle. Breathing the words in a low voice, almost sighing to himself, "Kâsim, here is your wife," he embraced the matting with great fervour, constantly repeating "My wife! my wife!" Some one said, "Kiss

her!" and he kissed her—repeatedly kissed her.
Then by another inspiration (I do not say from
whence), some one brought up the other Kâsim,
and introducing him to the other side of the roll
of matting, said, also very quietly, "Kâsim, this
is *your* wife!" and Kâsim the elder accepted
the providential appearance of his greatly-desired
spouse, and embraced her with not less fervour
than his namesake and rival.

It was evident that neither intended to give up
the lady to the other, and as each tried to monopolise
her charms a struggle began between them to obtain
complete possession, during which the audience,
almost frantic with delight, urged the actors in this
drama to manifest their affection to the lady of their
choice. In the midst of this clamour the Kâsims
and their joint spouse fell down, and as they nearly
rolled into the fire and seemed disinclined even
then to abandon the lady, she was taken away
and put back in her corner with the chairs and
snakes.

It is a detail, which I only add because some
readers hunger for detail, that neither of the Kâsims
possessed a wife.

I do not pretend to offer any explanation of the
cause of this state of mind which Malays call *lâtah*.

I imagine it is a nervous disease affecting the brain but not the body.

I have never met a medical man who has interested himself in the matter, and I cannot say whether the disease, if it be one, is curable or not— I should doubt it.

I have somewhere read that individuals similarly affected are found amongst the Canadian lumbermen.

# X

# THE ETERNAL FEMININE

Le bonheur de saigner sur le cœur
d'un ami

PAUL VERLAINE

THERE was a woman of Kelantan named Siti Maämih ; she was born of the people, neither good nor beautiful, nor attractive, nor even young, as youth goes in the East, but she had chosen to ally herself to a white man whom I will call Grant.

I know nothing of these two, but that he had work far away in a Malay jungle and she shared his loneliness, herself a stranger in that country. It was apparently an arrangement formed for mutual advantage, like many others of a more permanent character. If the connection began without any semblance of romance, it more than satisfied the expectations of the contracting parties, and when the moment of trial came the highest affection and the most sacred bond could hardly have suggested a greater sacrifice than this woman offered.

Whilst these two were living their unattractive lives there came difficulties between white man and brown—not specially between this white man and any with a darker skin : the quarrel was between white authority and Malay resentment of interference. Grant was not even remotely connected with the matter, but he was white, and under such circumstances a want of discrimination is not uncommon. There followed what is known as "a state of reprisals." Uncivilised people, who do not understand fine distinctions in such matters, called it war. The disturbance was, however, comparatively local, Grant's immediate neighbourhood did not seem affected, and he was probably unconcerned. Therefore he went about his work and took no special precaution, fearing no attack.

But his hut was isolated, there was only one other white man anywhere near him, no police within miles, and Maämih, who understood Malays better than her protector, was on the watch for trouble.

To expect is, sometimes, to go half way to meet, and the trouble came quickly.

One morning two Malays appeared at Grant's house, and, having given some trivial excuse for their presence and looked about the premises, took their departure. There was nothing unusual in that, and only a very nervous person would have seen in so simple an event any cause for alarm. But even ere this, prudence would have told most white men under similar circumstances that it would be well to see to their arms and keep them handy. Grant, however, took no precautions, as he had probably convinced himself that none were necessary ; as for arms, he does not appear to have had any.

That morning, or it may have been the evening before, three large boats and two small ones arrived in the river close by, but kept out of sight of Grant's hut, and he probably did not know they were there. They belonged to a minor chief who had no connection with the Malays then in arms.

The day wore on, Grant had been out all morning looking after his work, he had returned to breakfast, been out again, and now he was back and had thrown himself down to rest, glad to get under shelter from the oppressive heat. He was a busy man and his work took him out of doors, but though he had been about all day he had seen and heard nothing to arouse his suspicions.

Seen nothing, certainly. That was not strange, it was a jungly place, and to be ten yards off in the jungle is as good, for those who seek concealment and know the jungle, as to be in another district. As for hearing anything, that too was most unlikely : the only people he could hear from were Malays, the only means of communication the Malay language, of which Grant knew very little, and the only condition on which information is to be obtained from Malays about Malays would be an intimacy with and respect for the threatened man to which Grant could hardly aspire. There must be some very powerful influence at work to induce a Muhammadan, who is not personally in danger, to tell a Christian that there is a Muhammadan plot against his life. Grant, at any rate, if he thought about it at all, could hardly expect that he, a new-comer, possessed friends who would do so much for him.

He was still resting when, about 4 P.M., a party of nearly twenty armed men suddenly appeared in front of the house and stood some fifty yards away, while two of them, carrying only the ordinary jungle knives, came up to the house and asked Grant if he wanted to buy fowls. He told the inquirers to take them to his servant, and got up as the Malays left him.

The men had no fowls, and instead of going to the servant's quarters they rejoined their companions, and the whole body advanced towards the house.

At this moment Maämih appeared, and instantly

divining that the strangers meant no good, she screamed out, "They are going to murder us." But Grant said that he and she had done no harm and the Malays could mean none, and, taking the woman with him, he went out of the house and a few steps forward to meet his assailants.

These last stopped some twenty yards from Grant and the woman, and she said, "What harm have we done?" The answer was "*Titah*"—it is by order of the Raja—and they told the woman to leave the infidel and go away. But she replied, "I shall stay with him."

Then several men said, "If you do not go, we will kill you as well as the white man."

Grant may not have understood this sentence of death on himself, he may not have realised how strangely the times were out of joint, that he who was the enemy of no man, who had done no wrong, who represented no cause, should suddenly, in the broad light of day, hear his own death sentence, and in the same breath learn that he was facing his executioners and his account with the world was closed. There was no time to think : instinct said, "There is Death," and doubtless instinct also said, "Death is disagreeable : shun it."

It is commonly reputed that there are people who

do not know what fear is ; to them in such a situation instinct no doubt suggests that death is a new and pleasant experience. With this man it was different ; as he saw here and there a gun raised and pointed at him from a distance of a few paces, he probably felt the fear of sudden and violent death, and if he was in any way responsible for what he did in that supreme moment his thought must have suggested that these men would not harm a woman of their own nationality and religion, for he took her in his arms.

A shot was fired, and the bullet shattered Maämih's left arm. Then, seeing what had happened, Grant put her behind him and two more shots were fired, one of which struck Grant in the breast, and saying, "They have killed me," he fell on his face to the ground.

A Malay rushed up with a heavy chopping knife, but the woman threw herself on the body and put her unwounded arm over Grant's neck to save him. The Malay's first blow inflicted a deep wound on Maämih's arm and made her loose her hold; the man then struck Grant a heavy blow on the back of the neck, but he was already dead.

The murderers took no further notice of the woman, except to try and rob her of the jewellery she wore, but they plundered the house, and having decapitated the dead man and otherwise mutilated his body, they threw the remains into the river and departed.

The woman was cared for by a countryman of her own until she could be removed to a hospital, where, after weeks of suffering, she recovered from her injuries.

The motive of this outrage was simply the desire of an individual and his small following to wipe out the white man, and as Grant's isolated position made him a specially easy prey, he fell a victim. His only European neighbour was also murdered by the same band. I know of no similar attack being made by Malays on a white man within modern times, and I question whether there is such another instance of a Malay woman's devotion—not that they are not capable of such self-sacrifice, I think they are, but the circumstances necessary to call it forth very seldom arise.

This woman realised what was going to happen before she left the shelter of the house, she had time after that to think, her life was not sought, she was told to go away and warned that if she did not separate herself from the white man she would share his fate. Moreover, she knew that no sacrifice of hers could save him, and more than all, as affecting her woman's nerves, she saw face to face the men with murder in their faces and the means to accomplish it in their hands.

The motive which kept Maämih by Grant's side and which led her, after receiving the first shot, to interpose herself between his body and the weapons of his foes, must have been as high as it was powerful. Just as there was nothing to fear by standing aside (for none would have blamed her), so there was nothing to hope from the forbearance of Grant's murderers, and that she did not also lose her life by her devotion to him was the accident of an ill-directed shot and a well-aimed blow which sought to sever the woman's arm and reach the neck it protected—the neck of a dead man.

United to the devotion which deemed no sacrifice too great for one she loved, was that other sort of courage which comes of knowledge and deliberate intention. No one can fail to admire the pluck which takes no thought of danger, the instinct which impels a wild beast to charge an enemy and probably achieve thereby its own destruction. Even then it can hardly be said that the sensation of fear has never been and cannot be experienced by the most formidable and gallant denizens of the forest and the desert.   All sportsmen know the contrary, and a child has put a tiger to flight by suddenly throwing a basket in the face of the beast.  Had the child run away, its death was probable, whereas it saved the life of an old man already in the tiger's clutches, and yet the child's action was not the result of courage but of fear.

This Malay woman, in whom the love of life was strong, and on whose nerves the horror and certainty of what awaited her must have had a terrifying effect, deliberately renounced safety, with that higher resolve which, vanquishing fear, faces the unknown in the spirit described by the Persian who, writing eight centuries ago, has found so worthy an interpreter in the author of the lines—

" So when the Angel of the darker Drink
At last shall find you by the river brink
And, offering his Cup, invite your Soul,
Forth to your Lips to quaff—
            You shall not shrink."

# XI

# IN THE NOON OF NIGHT

Her soul upheld
By some deep-working charm
KIRKE WHITE

O N the western coast of the Peninsula, more especially that part of it which forms one side of the Straits of Malacca, the shore-line is generally one long stretch of mud, covered with mangrove trees to the verge of high-water mark and rather further, for when the tide is up there are thousands of acres of mangrove whose roots and several inches of the stems are submerged. Beyond this forest the receding tide leaves great wastes of evil-smelling mire, soft and clinging, in which the searcher for shell-fish sinks almost to his waist.

Many rivers, small and great, find their way to the sea through this wide flat. At high water they look imposing enough, but when the tide is out a narrow and shallow channel is left winding about

between low slimy banks, and right and left the eye
wanders over a desolation of glistening mud with an
almost imperceptible slope to the edge of the distant
sea.

Pools of shallow water and tiny channels, through
which the receding tide finds easier road to river
or sea, alone break the monotony of the unsightly
waste.

That is as far as physical features go.   The
mud-flats have their denizens, but they are not over-
attractive.

First, there is the Malay fisherman, hunting for
mussels and other shell-fish.   If he is there at all
he will be hard to see, for he pushes his little dug-
out fifty or a hundred yards up a mud creek, leaves
it and fossicks about, sunk above his knees in the
mire.

Then there are myriads of birds, attracted by the
great possibilities of gain to the industrious searcher
after garbage, stranded fish, and all sorts of particularly loathsome-looking and foul-smelling dead things
to be found in such a place.   These birds are often
strange-looking creatures, vast of size, long and lank
of leg, snaky of neck and spiky of bill.   But they
are wary to a degree, they always seems to be standing just in the tiny ripple of the smallest wavelets

where you instinctively know the mud and sea meet, and there they watch the gradually receding tide with melancholy abstraction, as though they took no real interest in the daily toil of sustaining life.

Last, there is something else here, and, if you are not quite a stranger, you will look first, look longest, and look always for this other thing. Perhaps it is the extraordinary fitness of her surroundings (I say *her* advisedly), perhaps the art with which nature has designed the body of the saurian to make you think her a log, or a stranded palm-branch, a half-buried spar of a wrecked boat, or even a lighter or darker ridge of the surrounding mud—certain it is that as the crocodile lies there, basking in the sun which makes air and water and blistering slime shimmer and dance before your eyes, you will not notice the creature, nay, even when pointed out to you, it is ten to one that you will not even then realise that she is there.

But get nearer, speak no word and let your rowers pull a long and noiseless stroke till some one with a quick eye and a steady hand can put a bullet in the reptile's neck. As that great mouth suddenly opens, disclosing the rows of shining teeth, as it shuts again with the noise of a steel trap, as the horrible scaly claws dig deep into the mud in their agony and the great spiked tail lashes round in fury, as the loathsome yellow belly slides over the ooze and you catch sight of the stony cruelty of the crocodile's eye, then you will realise what manner of thing she is, and you will probably conceive for her and all her kind a deadly horror and loathing, and a consuming desire to slay the whole brood will seize you then and remain with you for all time.

If it should happen to you to have to fight a wounded crocodile at close quarters, if accident brings you in contact with a man who has just lost arm or leg, or with a corpse out of which a crocodile has torn the life, your feelings towards these river-murderers will not be softened.

There are Malay rivers so infested by these reptiles that at low water for a mile or two from the river's mouth they will be seen, in twos and threes or larger groups, lying on either bank basking or sleeping in the sun. It repeatedly happens that they knock people out of their boats and then kill and devour them, and in places where the creatures are specially numerous, if a crocodile is shot dead on the bank, in less than half an hour the carcase will be dragged into the river and a crowd of the reptiles will be tearing it in pieces and fighting for the remains.

Villages on the Malay coast are nearly always situated on the bank of a river ; the sea is full of fish and the men of a coast village are mostly fishermen. If the village is of any size and the industry of any importance, the catching of fish is supplemented by curing—that is, salting and drying them.

The whereabouts of a village of this kind may be recognised by the traveller on sea or land when he is yet a great way off. Probably for that reason, and because the cleaning of thousands of fish loads the water with food of a kind that is specially attractive to the saurian, the immediate neighbourhood of a fishing village is the favourite resort of the crocodile.

At the mouth of a wide river on the Perak coast there is just such a village. It is thriving, and as there are a number of Chinese as well as Malay fishermen, it boasts a police-station. The houses are built for the most part on piles ; at high water the sea washes under them, and the means of intercommunication are wooden stagings from house to house. At low water there is mud, great stretches of mud, running from the edge of the mangrove swamp which backs the village far out to the west and the waters of the Straits of Malacca.

# IN THE NOON OF NIGHT

It was in the month of Ramthân, when begin those forty days of fast observed by all good Muhammadans—though so few of them know why they fast, or the details of the touching story which tells the sufferings of the Martyrs of Kerbela—that one night, past the middle of the month, but when the moon still lit up the water and made things plain as day, a strange thing happened at this small coast village.

In it there lived a Malay revenue officer with his wife and child, and on the night in question these three, being at home, went to sleep about 10 P.M. as was their wont.

A slight breeze was blowing off the sea, blowing against the falling tide, and the moonlight glorified the hideous expanse of slime till it looked like a limitless mirror, blending far away with the haze-enshrouded waters of the sea, but bordered landwards by that dark fringe of mangroves, the thick forest forming a striking contrast to the moonlit beauty of the glistening shore.

The wind sighed up the river, played through the great brown nets hanging up to dry, and, scarcely stirring the tops of the mangroves, swept gently towards the distant hills.

All the village slept, except the one Guardian of

the Peace, who showed his devotion to duty by punctually striking the hours on a huge metal gong.

The night was far advanced, when suddenly he heard a child crying in the house of the Malay revenue clerk. Then there was the noise of foot-steps and the voice of the man calling to his wife, but no answer. After a few minutes there was the sound of approaching feet, a shout from the Malay, followed by the man himself.

The constable called out, "What is the matter, Che Mat?"

Che Mat replied, "I was asleep, but awoke hear-ing the child crying for its mother. I could not see her anywhere, and she did not answer when I spoke. Then I got up and saw at once the door of the house was open, but she is nowhere to be seen. Have you heard anything of her?"

The constable had heard nothing, but there was evidently something uncanny about this disappear-ance, for, in a village such as this, where the houses are more in the water than on land, where the path-less mangrove is the background, and the waters of the river the foreground, there are few places left in which to look for any one or anything with any chance of finding them.

The man on guard roused his comrades, and, as

Malays do not sit down and discuss plans of action, some one at once made a move ; the others followed, and they all walked out to the last house on the platform, and then listened.

"Hark! did you not hear something?" Yes, through the silence of the night, wafted on the incoming breeze, there was a distinct but faint cry from the direction of the sea.

It did not take the men long to get down to the ground, and first hurrying along the edge of the trees, they went some distance, hearing the cries at intervals and ever more plainly, till it became necessary to strike right out across the mud. By this time there was no doubt about the source of the cries, for the voice of the object of their search was recognised, and that the woman was in sore distress did not admit of doubt. Making all the speed they could, sinking above their knees at every step, stumbling, falling, but ever pressing on, they saw at last to their horror, in the brilliant moon-light, the woman on the ground being literally worried by three crocodiles, each six or eight feet in length.

As crocodiles go, six or eight feet is no great length, but to go to sleep in your own house and wake up at midnight within a hundred feet of the

L. r'

sea, but with half a mile of mud between you and anything like dry land, and at the same time assailed by *three* crocodiles quite big enough to kill you, is calculated to shock the strongest nerves.

After a short but exciting fight, the police beat off the scaly beasts with difficulty, and found the woman had been badly torn in legs, and arms, and neck.

Whilst the men were arranging to carry her back, no easy matter over half a mile of soft but sticky wet mud and ooze, she told her tale :

" I was sleeping," she said, " and had a vision. Two radiant Beings appeared to me and bid me rise and follow them, and they would show me a sight more glorious than is vouchsafed to mortals. Transported with joy, I rose and followed them, and whilst filled with ecstatic rapture by the companionship of these Celestial Beings, I seemed to be borne along without effort of my own through enchanted fields of more than earthly beauty. Suddenly I was awakened by feeling the teeth of a crocodile in my leg, and, to my horror, I found I was out here on this mud-flat half a mile from home, but close to the sea, with three crocodiles attacking me, no means of defending myself, and little hope of help. I fell, and the beasts tore and worried me, biting my arms, and legs, and neck, while I screamed for help until you came and rescued me."

Well, after all, there is nothing very strange in that. A woman of peculiar nervous organisation, a somnambulist, dreams a dream and walks out into the balmy atmosphere of a moonlit Eastern night. She walks rather far, and has a rude awakening. That is nothing ; other sleepers have walked further, and their awakening has been to the life beyond the grave.

Only this was curious : that while the men sank deep into the mud at every step, the woman had never sunk in at all. When found, there was only mud on the *soles* of her feet, and, though she had walked half a mile across the flat, and her tracks were plainly visible in the moonlight, they were all on the surface, and she had crossed the soft, unstable mire as easily as though it had been a metalled road.

So the men bore her home, not wondering over-much, for in this thing they saw the hand of the Celestial Beings who guided her feet with such consideration, to abandon her to the ferocious attentions of the crocodiles.

The woman herself, her husband, and the police were satisfied as to the means, but found the end too hard for their understanding.

The ideal woman, the product of higher education and deep research in divers subjects, supplies
the real clue to the phenomenon, for, when asked
"where the true Spirit of God is," she modestly
replies, "I can tell you : it is in us *women*. We
have preserved it and handed it down from one
generation to another of our own sex unsullied."*

Doubtless—from the time when the Spirit moved
upon the face of the waters, and, later, on the Sea
of Galilee ; but it is more difficult to understand how
woman, unaided, has handed anything down from
one generation to another.

The same idea is, however, more happily conveyed in the injunction of the President of the
Scraggsville Woman's Suffrage League to her
husband, when ordering him to go and purchase a
divided skirt. "If you are afraid, pray to God for
courage ; *She* will help you."

The mere male has his uses, one of which is to
assist the unsullied sex to perpetuate the Spirit of
God, and another to be within hail when there are
crocodiles about.

* "The Heavenly Twins," book iii., chap. iii.

# XII

# VAN HAGEN AND CAVALIERO

How loved, how honoured once, avails
thee not,
To whom related, or by whom begot,
A heap of dust alone remains of thee
POPE

NOT many months after my first arrival in the East I met, in a club in Singapore, an Italian called Cavaliero. He was quite young, tall, dark, and good-looking, of a pronounced Italian type. What his occupation was I have no idea; I suppose he had some sort of business, but it could not have been very attractive or profitable, for one day I was told that he and a Hollander named Van Hagen had collected about a hundred natives of all sorts and conditions and had accepted service with the Viceroy of the Sultan of Selangor.

Selangor was then an absolutely independent Malay State, so independent in fact that the principal and almost only employment of its inhabitants was fighting.

The Sultan was and is an old gentleman for whom I have the highest regard, and I desire to speak of him with the greatest respect. He had had his own fighting day and was tired of it, he wished to be left alone, that was all; but he recognised that boys will be boys, and if the young Selangor Rajas took their pleasure in this way, he was inclined to regard their escapades with an indulgent eye, provided they did not interfere with his *opium cum dignitate* and his immediate surroundings.

The Sultan's own sons were very much interested in the guerilla warfare that was then being carried on throughout Selangor, and the feature of the disturbances was that every chief said he had the Sultan's approval of his proceedings. Some time later I was myself in Selangor, and, as this statement was constantly being dinned into my ears, I took the liberty of asking his Highness what it meant.

He promptly pointed out that each of these Rajas in turn came to him, stated his case, and asked the Sultan if that was not correct. His Highness always replied, "Quite correct," but, as he explained to me, "*bĕnar ka-pâda dia, bûkan bĕnar ka-pâda kami,*" which being interpreted means, "correct in their view, not in mine." He was evidently tickled by this happy inspiration and laughed heartily at his own ingenuity.

The gossips declared that his Highness was always requested to give a tangible proof of his approval in the shape of gunpowder and lead, and that he gave them to every applicant with strict impartiality. On this point the Sultan told me nothing, and I was not indiscreet enough to inquire, but as Selangor is no more free from gossip than its neighbours, I put the statement down to irresponsible chatter.

All this is, however, by the way. Certain Rajas held certain important strategical points from which other Rajas kept trying to oust them, and the fight waxed hottest about Klang, the principal port of the State, and Kuala Lumpor, the principal mining centre.

As to Klang, it had just been captured by a notable warrior named Raja Mahdi, and its whilom defenders driven out when the Sultan gave his only daughter in marriage to Tunku dia Udin, brother of the Sultan of Kedah. The Sultan's son-in-law espoused the cause of those who had been driven from Klang, and, as he was created Viceroy and had powerful support in Singapore, matters were further complicated.

The Viceroy and his friends recovered possession of Klang and secured the friendship and assistance of the Chinese miners at Kuala Lumpor.

These Chinese were led by one Ah Loi, a remarkable man, styled the "Capitan China," whose instincts were distinctly warlike and his authority with his countrymen supreme.

Raja Mahdi also had friends who were acting against the Chinese in the interior, and supporters outside the State who helped him with money, stores, and arms, and thus the ball rolled merrily along.

Dame Fortune was, as usual, fickle, and success was now with the Viceroy and now with Mahdi and his friends. The Capitan China did his share in his own way. He offered fifty silver dollars for every enemy's head delivered in the market-place in front of his house at Kuala Lumpor, and he told me himself that his man who stood there ready to receive the hideous trophies and pay the money did quite a brisk business.

As with all Malay war, the operations languished and revived by fits and starts. Plenty of money meant plenty of men, arms, and ammunition, and with them a spasmodic effort would be made and probably a success gained. Then would follow dire scarcity, and the other side, having raised some money, would in their turn gain an advantage.

Thus the tide of battle ebbed and flowed for months and years, and the only plain and evident result was that the population of Selangor was rapidly diminishing, the ground in the immediate neighbourhood of Kuala Lumpor town being thickly planted with corpses, for there the battle was always the hottest, both because of the Capitan China's special method and because of the value of the mines. The survivors on both sides were not only being reduced to penury, but their leaders were becoming involved in debts which only the complete success of one side followed by lasting peace and order could enable the victors to pay from the revenues derived from the tin-mines. The debts of the defeated would naturally be irrecoverable.

While the State was distracted by all this trouble the Sultan still secured a comparative tranquillity by his diplomatic sympathy with the combatants, and whichever side held the Klang custom-house supplied him with funds. That was the price of his qualified approval.

It was at this time that the Viceroy's party, being in funds, conceived the plan of raising a force in

Singapore with which they hoped to deal an effective blow to their enemies.

I have said I knew little of Cavaliero, but of Van Hagen, who took command of the recruits, I know less. I was told that he had been an officer in the Netherlands army, and that he lost his commission owing to some breach of discipline, but that he was a man of birth, character, and courage.

His heterogeneous force, composed of natives of half-a-dozen nationalities, went by sea to Klang, disembarked and made its way with guides through the jungle to Kuala Lumpor. There they stockaded themselves on a hill above the town and did valiantly in its defence. But the place was invested by the enemy, supplies were cut off, and while the force was daily harassed by the fire from the enemy's works, provisions ran short and the men were threatened at once with starvation and the probability of being surrounded and entirely cut off from their base at Klang, twenty-five miles distant by a jungle track.

Under these circumstances, and probably moved by the growing discontent of their men, Van Hagen and Cavaliero determined, ere it should be too late, to endeavour to make their way back to the port.

They were all strangers in the country, and they

could find no one to guide them through the jungle, but their difficulties became so great that they decided to risk the journey as a choice of evils, and early one morning they set out.

I have elsewhere tried to describe a Malay jungle, and the path which these men had to traverse was, as I know from my own experience, beset with peculiar difficulty, and led for a great deal of the way through swamp and water, where, of course, there was no track visible. It is not surprising that the party lost its way. Not only that, but weak from want of food, wanting in cohesion and discipline, and with the knowledge that they were seeking blindly for a road unknown to all, a feeling of despair overcame many of them, and they wandered off in different directions never to be seen or heard of again.

The main body, with Van Hagen and Cavaliero, after a weary day's march and no food, arrived in the evening, utterly exhausted, at a place called Patâling, only four miles from Kuala Lumpor! They had been walking in a circle, and had got back to a point not far from that of their original departure.

Patâling was held by a considerable body of the enemy under two Malay Rajas, and the weary wanderers walked straight into their arms and gave themselves up without a struggle.

Another story says that, at the last moment before leaving Kuala Lumpor, a guide presented himself and offered his services, which were accepted; that he led the party hither and thither through the jungle, and in the evening, when thoroughly exhausted, took them into Patâling.

I never heard rightly what became of the rank and file; they may have been given their liberty and told to find their own way out of the State. For the officers was reserved another fate.

Finding the principal defenders of Kuala Lumpor had withdrawn, the place was occupied without difficulty by those who had for so long invested it. The leading Chinese were made very uncomfortable, but on them depended the working of the mines, and they were allowed to purchase their lives.

I do not think this alternative was offered to Van Hagen and Cavaliero. They were escorted from Patâling to Kuala Lumpor, and, arrived there, they were taken out and shot.

In excavating for the foundations of the houses which now form the town of Kuala Lumpor, it was usual to dig up a large number of skeletons, the bones of those who had fallen during the years of Selangor's internecine strife. As many as sixteen skeletons have been discovered in digging out the foundations for one house.

One day, not many years ago, two skeletons were thus discovered. The bones were larger, the figures taller, than those usually met with. They were the skeletons of two men face to face, and locked in each other's arms.

# XIII

# THE PASSING OF PĔNGLIMA PRANG SĔMAUN

Oh vengeance ! thou art sweet

LEWIS MORRIS

ON the Perak River, about fifty miles from its mouth, and just above the tidal influence, where the water is clear and shallow and the banks are lined with palm groves and orchards, there is a large Malay village called Bandar.

More than twenty years ago there dwelt in this village a man named Mĕgat Raja, married to a particularly well-favoured girl named Mĕriam. The fact of her marriage drew her into some sort of notoriety, and her attractions were soon the gossip of the place. The gilded youths of Bandar were fired by the description of Mĕriam's charms, and one of them, a boy of good family, position, and means, got sight of and fell in love with her.

The husband, Mĕgat Râja, was conveniently called away to accompany the Sultan on a journey to Penang and Che Nuh, the youth aforesaid, profiting by that opportunity, pushed his addresses with such fervour and success that he became the lady's lover.

Late one night when Che Nuh was in the house of his mistress, Mĕgat Râja unexpectedly returned and the first the lovers knew of their danger was the demand of the husband to be admitted. The house was a large one enclosed by a palisade, and Mĕriam thus suddenly surprised, and fearing instant death if her husband should discover Che Nuh, implored her lover to escape by the door at the back of the house while that at the front was being opened.

Che Nuh complied, but the husband had evidently heard something of what had been going on in his absence, and, as the lover was about to descend the steps, he drew back seeing Mĕgat Râja waiting on the ground beneath them.

He drew back, but not before his presence had been perceived.

Mĕgat Râja called out "Who is that?"

Che Nuh replied "It is I, Che Nuh."

The husband, drawing his *kris*, said "What are

you doing in my house at this time? Come down on to the ground."

Mat Nuh was alone and Měgat Râja was accompanied by two other men, but the youth unsheathed his *kris* and went down ready to accept the chances of a hand-to-hand struggle.

Seeing that Mat Nuh would defend himself, and knowing that he was no contemptible adversary, the three men hesitated. What was of more account in their minds was that Che Nuh belonged to a powerful family, and his father was one of the principal chiefs in the country. There was, therefore, the certainty of retaliation should they kill him, and the uncertainty of his guilt, for Měriam was not the only woman in the house. As the men stood mutually on the defensive, Měgat Râja asked him whom he had come to see, and Che Nuh replied that it was a girl in the house. Thinking to assure himself on this point, the husband entered the house and questioned one of the servant-women, but dissatisfied with what he heard he dashed out again determined to attack Che Nuh.

The latter had, however, taken advantage of Měgat Râja's momentary absence to get outside the gate of the palisade, and once there he shouted for help and was soon surrounded by his friends.

In reply to a call, Che Nuh bid his adversary come outside the gate and he would give him any satisfaction he pleased.

That of course meant an internecine struggle between the two parties, and Mĕgat Râja declined it, for the odds were now against him, and he was still uncertain whether his wife were unfaithful or not.

On the strong suspicion that he held, his inclination was to at least make short work of the woman, but here again he was deterred by the knowledge that her relations would certainly be revenged on him. He, therefore, decided on another course of action. On the assumption that his wife was guilty (and of this he became tolerably well assured), he treated her as though he held the proofs, divorced her, turned her out of his house, and declined to let her have any of her own possessions or to remove any of his.

This action was considered a very serious indignity by Mĕriam's friends, and it so happened that she possessed a relative named Pĕnglima Prang Sĕmaun, an adherent of the Sultan's Wazïr, the Râja Bĕndahâra, and he was reputed one of the principal warriors in the country.

Pĕnglima Prang Sĕmaun called upon the Chief of

Bandar and laid a formal complaint against Měgat Râja, demanding to know why he had taken the law into his own hands and treated Měriam in a manner to put all her relatives to shame.

The Chief of the village of Bandar was also one of the great officers of State named the Orang Kâya Shabandar. He was a man renowned for his courage, was wealthy, a trusted officer of the Sultan, the receiver of customs, and lived at the upper end of the village.

He listened politely to Pěnglima Prang Sěmaun, and when the latter wound up his complaint by saying he would certainly attack Měgat Râja if he obtained no redress, the Shabandar put his advice in the form of this ancient saw :

" If you have no gold, it is well to sing small ; if you have no pivot-guns (jingals), it is well to put a pleasant face on the matter ; and if you have no cannon, it is better to be quiet."

The advice was meant in good part and not as a taunt, but Pěnglima Prang Sěmaun took it as the latter and retired with rage in his heart, saying " It is well for you who have gold and jingals and cannon to tell me I have none of these things, but I will have my revenge of you with only a *kris*."

Then he returned to his own home to think how this was to be worked out.

The Pĕnglima Prang Sĕmaun's house was between those of the Shabandar, up stream, and Mĕgat Râja, down stream, and he knew that he was not strong enough to resist a combined attack from both of them. Therefore he determined that force must be backed by cunning if he was to achieve his end. He concluded that his only plan was to attack the Shabandar, dispose of him first as the most important, and then deal with Mĕgat Râja at his leisure.

Meanwhile, Che Nuh had expressed his desire to marry Mĕriam, but as his relatives recognised that such an open avowal of his *liaison* must lead to trouble with Mĕgat Râja and his folk, they declined to allow him to do this, and Che Nuh's negative attitude towards the lady only increased the wrath of her kinsman, Pĕnglima Prang Sĕmaun.

I have said that this bravo, for that was his *métier*, was the henchman of the Râja Bĕndahâra, the highest authority in the State after the Sultan. Pĕnglima Prang Sĕmaun, having determined to kill the Shabandar, felt it necessary to report the intention to his master and, mindful of possible wrath to come, to ask his sanction.

Accordingly the Pĕnglima went up river to Blanja where the Bĕndahâra lived, told his tale and asked for leave to kill the Shabandar.

The reply of the Bĕndahâra was, " If you think you are able to do it, go on."

That was enough. Pĕnglima Prang Sĕmaun returned to Bandar with a kindred spirit named Haji Ali, another bravo of reputation as evil as his own, and these two worthies soon settled their plan of operations.

The Sultan was at Pâsir Panjang (only a few miles above Bandar), with a large following and a crowd of boats, and the Pĕnglima and his friend determined to wreak their vengeance on the Shabandar on the *Râya Hâji*, the day to which the most religious Muhammadans prolong the fast of Ramthân.

The day did not, however, suit, there were too many people constantly about the Shabandar's house, and the conspirators had to return home without effecting their purpose.

On the following day, however, in the afternoon, Pĕnglima Prang Sĕmaun, Haji Ali, and three others, made a formal visit to the Shabandar, obtained admission to his house, and found in it no one besides himself and a Sumatran Râja, a visitor from down river. I say no one else but, as Pĕnglima Prang well knew, there were in the Shabandar's house two aged ladies, the mother of the Sultan's children and her sister.

The five men waited until they saw the Sumatran Râja take his departure, and in order to do this visitor honour, the Shabandar unarmed and un-attended, accompanied him to the river-bank and there bid him farewell.

This was the moment for the development of the plot.

Pĕnglima Prang Sĕmaun took leave of the Sha-bandar and shook hands with him. Haji Ali, a very big powerful man, then also took leave and grasped the Shabandar's hand, but instead of letting it go he drew the Dâtoh towards him, and the reply to his question of what this meant was a stab in the back from Pĕnglima Prang Sĕmaun's *kris*.

The blade did not pierce the skin, it bent, and the thrust was repeated with the same result, Haji Ali all the while holding the unarmed man by the hand.

Then the Pĕnglima threw away the useless weapon, and, seizing another *kris*, plunged it time after time into the helpless body of the Shabandar, who fell to the ground, while Haji Ali and each of the others stabbed him in turn.

Leaving the body lying on the bank, the men rushed straight back into the house, shut the gates of the enclosure and immediately prepared to defend themselves, taking particular care that the two ladies already mentioned should not get away.

The news of a murder perpetrated like this is carried on the breeze, and for a few minutes the Shabandar's adherents rushed up one after the other to be slaughtered as they arrived by the Pĕnglima and his party reinforced by their own men who had been awaiting the *dénoûement*.

Then gates and doors were closed, windows barred, cannon, pivot-guns, and muskets loaded, and Pĕnglima Prang Sĕmaun having rifled the house (which contained the customs collections as well as the Shabandar's private property), and thus possessed himself of all those things which he previously lacked, sat down to calmly await the development of events.

The plot had been cunningly conceived. The brutal murder of the unarmed chief was certain to be instantly avenged, and that would have been done by an attack on the house had it not been that it contained, besides the murderers, the Sultan's late wife and her sister, who were wellnigh sure to come to harm in the assault.

The risk of that possibility deterred the Sultan's people, who had surrounded the house with stockades, and all that could be done was to prevent the Pĕnglima, Haji Ali, and their men, from escaping. The process of starving out the besieged could not be resorted to, for here also the ladies would have suffered.

The moment the deed was done, Pĕnglima Prang Sĕmaun proclaimed that he was merely the instrument of the Sultan's Wazîr, and that he had acted on the authority of the Râja Bĕndahâra. That, if true, complicated the case considerably, and as matters had arrived at an *impasse*, a parley was called, and it was arranged that the Pĕnglima and his people should be given a safe-conduct to the Sultan at Pâsir Panjang.

Accordingly, the Pĕnglima Prang, Haji Ali, and the others left their shelter and embarked in boats provided for them, but they took good care not to let the ladies, who were their prisoners, get out of reach.

Arrived at Pâsir Panjang, Pĕnglima Prang at once sent a messenger to the Râja Bĕndahâra to inform him of the state of affairs and ask his aid. The Bĕndahâra responded to this appeal by taking boat, and, with a great following, descended the river to Pâsir Panjang. Once there, he availed himself of an ancient custom called *îkat-diri*—that is, to " bind yourself "—and, accompanied by all his people, he went and stood in front of the Sultan's house with his hands loosely tied behind his back with his own head-kerchief, and, thus uncovered in the sun, he and all his following shouted *âmpun Tûan-ku, be-rîbu-rîbu âmpun*—" Pardon, my lord, a thousand-thousand pardons."

After a quarter of an hour's waiting, while the air was filled with this plea for mercy, and the Bĕndahâra and his company stood like prisoners in front of the closed house, a door opened, a herald bearing the Sultan's insignia appeared and cried out : "Our lord pardons you, and permits you to enter into his presence."

That settled the affair. The Sultan's minister had accepted the responsibility for what had been done ; he was far too great a man to be treated as a criminal, and, taking advantage of an old custom, he confessed his fault, offered himself a prisoner, sought and obtained the Sultan's pardon.

Amongst those who had received the message of peace, and who entered into the presence, were the Pĕnglima Prang Sĕmaun, Haji Ali, and the three other murderers of the Shabandar.

Now, the Shabandar had a brother, and he was a man of war, and the Sultan well knew that this method of dealing with the murderers would not satisfy him, so he at once created him Dâtoh Shabandar in succession to the dead man, in the hope that the gift of this dignity might make for the general peace.

The Râja Bĕndahâra, accompanied by Pĕnglima Prang and his friends, then returned to Blanja.

The new Shabandar had no intention of leaving his brother's murderers to boast of their exploit, and, in a very short time, he asked for the Sultan's permission to attack them and wipe out the disgrace of his relative's unavenged death.

The Sultan said the request must be preferred to the Râja Bĕndahâra, for so long as the Pĕnglima Prang was in his village he could not be attacked without the Wazîr's sanction. Application was duly made to the Bĕndahâra, who replied that it would be contrary to custom to attack the Pĕnglima Prang while living at his door, but that if they could get him away they might do what they pleased.

The Pĕnglima Prang was, however, far too wary to be lured away from safety, and matters were in this state when there returned from a pilgrimage to

Mecca a man called Haji Mûsah, nearly related to the late Shabandar.

Haji Mûsah was at this time a rather small, spare man of middle age, but his heart was out of proportion to the size of his body, and when he heard what had recently taken place in Bandar, and how Pĕnglima Prang Sĕmaun and Haji Ali had got away unpunished, his anger knew no bounds.

He promptly waited upon the Sultan and begged for permission to attack the Pĕnglima, and, if necessary, to include in the operations his protector, the Râja Bĕndahâra.

The Sultan hesitated to give the desired permission, but the fact that the proposal had been made very soon reached Blanja and the ears of both the Wazîr and Pĕnglima Prang. Whatever the latter was he could not be accused of cowardice, and he at once offered to anticipate an attack by making an expedition against Haji Mûsah to silence so arrogant a foe.

The Râja Bĕndahâra enraged at the idea that his name should have been mentioned with so little respect, and apprehensive that Haji Mûsah might find the means (as he knew he had the will) to carry out his suggestion, cordially approved the Pĕnglima's proposal.

It did not take long to collect from the neighbouring village of Lambor enough men to fill two
boats, and, as that was all the Pĕnglima wanted for
his purpose, the party had started for Bâtak Râbit
(Haji Mûsah's village) before the down-stream
people had the smallest inkling of their intention.
The time was specially well chosen from the fact
that the Shabandar was absent in a remote district.

In Japan they say, "If you have not seen Nikko
you cannot say *gekko*," and if there is anyone who
knows the Malay Peninsula and yet has never
watched the sun set across the rice-fields, when
the ripe grain hangs heavily in the ear, his knowledge of the beauties of Malay scenery is very in-
complete.

A wide, flat plain covered by the golden harvest,
the rice-stalks standing five or six feet above the
ground from which they have sucked all the water
which nourished them in the earlier stages of
growth. One yellow sea of yellow ears, the green
stalks only discernible in the near foreground.

This sea is broken by islands of palms and fruit-
trees in which nestle the picturesque brown huts of
cottagers, houses of wood, built on wooden piles
with palm-thatched roofs and mat walls.

The setting sun strikes in great beams of saffron

light across this wide expanse of grain bounded by distant ranges of soft blue hills. How greedily one drinks it all in! and, as the Eye of Day droops lower, there shoot from between its closing lids rays of fire which tinge the glistening palms with a rosy effulgence, followed all too soon by the pale opalescent shades which proclaim the approach of the fast-driving chariot of night.

A grey haze rises from the damp earth, spreads in thin wreaths across the darkening plain, thickens to a heavy dead-white vapour, and as the silver sickle rises over the distant hills it shines upon clustered plumes of dark fronds mysteriously poised above a motionless drift of snow-like cloud.

On the edge of such a field was the home of Haji Mûsah. Behind stretched the rich plain, in front a great river, both wide and deep, its banks lined by groves of coco-nuts in the neighbourhood of villages, but elsewhere covered by forest and the *nipah* palm.

The dwelling stood a few feet back from the river, and, as its owner was a man of means, the structure was of some size, the floor and walls of stout planks and a strong palisade enclosed the surrounding yard. The house was, as usual, on wooden piles, and the kitchen, also on piles but separated from the main building, was connected with it by a platform.

It was here that Pĕnglima Prang Sĕmaun, Haji Ali, and the rest of their crew arrived one morning before daylight and quickly landed under the cover of darkness.

The enterprise they had undertaken was a perilous one. Their force numbered about thirty men all told, they had come about ninety miles right into the heart of the enemy's country, and, if there were any failure, retreat was a choice between a return against the current with a hostile people on either bank, or a long pull to the river's mouth under the same conditions and then the sea.

Pĕnglima Prang Sĕmaun had, however, calculated the chances, and he counted on a successful surprise and, if need be, the pursuit of those tactics which he had already, at Bandar, found so useful.

Once on shore the palisade of Haji Mûsah's house was cautiously approached, and, the gate being locked, it was scaled, and the whole party noiselessly established themselves beneath the house and waited for daylight.

It so happened that the house contained only two men and two women—Haji Mûsah and his wife,

Haji Hawah, and their daughter and son-in-law, the latter named Haji Sâhil.

At daybreak the back door of the house was opened and the two women came out and went into the kitchen. In a moment Haji Hawah discovered that the space beneath the house was full of armed men, and with a scream she rushed back towards the door. Ere she could gain it, Haji Ali sprang upon the platform and seized one of her hands, while her husband, unpleasantly alive to the situation, caught hold of the other and tried to pull her within the door, an effort which she seconded with all her might.

A real tug-of-war was carried on for a few moments, and Haji Ali was joined by another man.

Local tradition says that Haji Ali experienced suddenly a feeling that something dire was going to happen, and he asked his companion to relieve him of his hold of the woman's hand. The man took it, and Haji Mûsah from the inside making a great effort drew his wife towards him, and at the same time, with a spear, thrust out beyond her with so true an aim that he transfixed her would-be captor. The man released his hold, fell with a groan into Haji Ali's arms, and Haji Mûsah, drawing his wife into the house and believing he had wounded Pĕnglima Prang Sĕmaun, shouted as he closed the door, "That has wetted you, Pĕnglima!"

Wetted him with blood.

Haji Ali called to the Pĕnglima, "Help me, a 'watering' has befallen our friend"; a polite way of expressing a disaster. By the time they got the man to the ground he was dead, for the spear had struck home.

The Pĕnglima, furious at this sight, leapt on the platform, and, finding the door immovable, dashed open a small side-window with the butt end of a musket and fired into the house, but hurt no one.

In the scuffle before the door was closed Haji Mûsah had accidentally given his son-in-law a flesh wound on the shoulder, and that had disabled him, so the defence of the position rested on one man alone.

Pĕnglima Prang Sĕmaun now summoned Haji Mûsah to surrender, but the reply was, "I will not surrender."

"Then," said the Pĕnglima, "I will riddle the house with bullets."

"Shoot away," was the reply.

"I will burn the house down."

"Burn it," said Haji Mûsah, "and do whatever else you like, but I will not give in." .

"Let us burn it," said the Pĕnglima. But Haji Ali protested. "Are you mad," he urged, "already our enemies are collecting outside, you would burn the house down and these people in it, and then what should we do? Caught like fish in a basket, without walls or roof to shelter us, what will become of us?"

The wisdom of this advice was apparent, and as it was necessary to deal with those in the house quickly the leader set to work to devise another plan.

An evil inspiration came to the Pĕnglima, and he told Haji Ali to get Haji Mûsah into conversation again while he, having loaded with all manner of missiles a pivot-gun which he found under the house, listened attentively to the sound of Haji Mûsah's voice, and tying the gun to a post just beneath the spot where he thought the Haji must be standing, fired it.

A large hole was rent in the floor, and, the various missiles scattering in all directions, one of them struck Haji Mûsah in the thigh, seriously wounding him and placing him *hors de combat*. His wife was also hit, but only slightly injured.

The assailants realised the effects of the shot from what they heard said within and again called

upon Haji Mûsah to yield, but he declined utterly
to do so.

His wife said, " What is the use, you are wounded
and cannot fight, so am I and so is Haji Sâhil, what
can we do, better make terms with them ? " Haji
Mûsah stubbornly declined to listen to this persua-
sion and only said, "Let them do their worst, I
will not yield."

Strange to say it was only then that Haji Hawah
realised that her daughter was missing. She
remembered that the girl had left the house with her
and gone into the kitchen, but until that moment,
what with the discovery that the enemy was within
their gates, the struggle at the door and subsequent
events, she had not thought of the girl further than
to suppose she was sitting terrified in some corner
of the never brilliantly lighted house.

Now, however, it was certain that she had failed
to get back before the door was closed and must
have fallen into the hands of the enemy.

As a matter of fact nothing of the kind had
happened. On the first alarm, seeing the crowd of
strange men and her mother's struggles to gain the
house, the girl was too terrified to leave her shelter
and had hidden herself in the kitchen. The enemy
being all under the house when the women first

came out, no one had particularly noticed the girl or ever thought of entering her hiding-place.

The moment Haji Hawah was convinced her daughter was not in the house, she became equally certain she was in the hands of the enemy, and that was an intolerable idea. She, therefore, besought her husband to offer to yield provided the girl were restored. This new factor in the case persuaded him, and Haji Mûsah called out that he would yield if his daughter were given back to them.

At first the besiegers could not understand the meaning of this proposal, but light very soon came to them and they argued that if the girl was not inside the house or in their hands, she must be in the kitchen, and a search of that place very soon discovered her.

The Pĕnglima accordingly replied that he accepted the proposal and would restore the girl on condition her father yielded. The door was then opened and the girl admitted, but no sooner was she in the house than it was closed again and Haji Mûsah declined to give himself up.

Shortly after, however, the loss of blood and pain of his stiffening limb made movement impossible and compelled Haji Mûsah to abandon all idea of further resistance.

The Pěnglima and his friends having gained the house proceeded to make themselves comfortable and did not attempt to disturb or annoy Haji Mûsah and his family.   These latter occupied a curtained portion of the principal room, and underneath their only window a sentry was placed night and day.

Meanwhile the Shabandar, informed by messenger of what had taken place, hurried back to the neighbourhood and reinforced the adherents of Haji Mûsah, who so far had contented themselves with building and occupying stockades to command Haji Mûsah's house.

The Pěnglima's tactics were again completely successful, and as it was impossible to fire on the captors without danger to their imprisoned friends the Shabandar, who now commanded the investing force, set himself to devise a plan whereby he might gain his end by craft.

The Pěnglima's men occupied the house and one or two small stockades close by it.  The Shabandar's party had built a series of enclosing works which practically cut off escape to landward.   In front was the river and here again, both up stream and down, there lay a small fleet of guard-boats.

The Pěnglima's own two boats were chained to the landing-stage where they were safe, for it would have been impossible to seize them without being exposed to fire from the house, to which no reply could be made.

A month went by, and in that time Haji Mûsah, his wife, and son-in-law had fairly recovered from their injuries. Meanwhile the Shabandar, by means of spies, learned that the prisoners occupied a side of the house where there was but one window, and that always guarded at night by the same man. Through this man there was the best chance of escape for the prisoners, if only he could be bought over.

This sentry, who had some authority over part of the band, was a foreigner, he was getting tired of the game and probably did not altogether like the outlook or see how his party was to turn the situation to their own advantage. At any rate communications were opened between the Shabandar and him, and for a sum of two thousand dollars he promised to get the prisoners out of the window and through the lines to their friends.

In the dead of a dark night (and moonless Eastern nights can be black as a sepulchre) he assisted the four prisoners to make their escape through the window, while the Pĕnglima, Haji Ali, and a number of their men slept peacefully on the other side of the sheltering curtain that gave privacy to the women.

Guided by the traitor, their movements hidden in Cimmerian darkness, the little party made its way in safety to the friendly shelter of the Shabandar's stockade. He was expecting them, and he had also prepared an unpleasant surprise for the cuckoos in temporary occupation of their stolen nest.

Pĕnglima Prang Sĕmaun and his friends were awakened from sleep by the banging of jingals and muskets and a hail of various missiles.

A moment's search showed that the prisoners had escaped, and the Pĕnglima instantly realised that he was in the toils.

He had already shown that he was a man of resource, and his presence of mind did not desert him in this dangerous crisis. The darkness alone protected them, and that would not last ; moreover, he could not tell at what moment his position might not be rushed. It was clear that for them was reserved the fate of those who when they got up in the morning were all dead men.

The Pĕnglima called his followers together, explained the situation and its urgency, pointed out the choice that lay before them—an attempt to pass the enemy's stockades under cover of the night or to run the gauntlet of the guard-boats, where capture was, as he said, certain.

The men of the band, the wretched Lambor contingent, elected, as the Pĕnglima had meant they should do, to try and force their way through the enemy's lines, never thinking that if they succeeded they would only reach a pathless jungle swamp, where they, strangers in that part of the country, must either perish miserably or return to the tender mercies of the investing foe.

Of these deplorable eventualities they took no thought; there was little time for hesitation; tightening the grasp upon their weapons they went out into the night, and in a few moments the shouts from the surrounding stockades showed that their intention had been discovered.

This was exactly what Pĕnglima Prang Sĕmaun had expected; he had created a diversion, and seizing his opportunity, accompanied by Haji Ali and a few of his particular associates, he made for the river and got into one of his boats, cast off and pulled out into the stream.

A very wily man was the Pĕnglima. Every one in the guard-boats was on the alert, the firing and shouts from the shore had warned them that the fox was being hunted in the covert, and the pack were after him in full cry. Still there was just a trifle of uncertainty about it, and that was the Pĕnglima's one chance of salvation.

The slightest hesitation now, the smallest of false steps, and neither the Pĕnglima nor any of those with him would ever see the dawn. He knew it well enough, and as he ordered those who had taken the oars to pull out boldly into the stream, he grasped the helm and steering straight up the middle of the river, *against* the tide, he gave orders that no man should speak, undertaking the whole responsibility himself.

It was still so dark that no one could see quite whence this boat came, or distinguish who was in it, but as it moved with plenty of noise and no attempt at concealment right towards the line of guard-boats, some one called out, " Who goes there ? "

"It is I," replied the Pĕnglima, "I bring the Shabandar's orders to you to keep a good look-out, they are attacking the Pĕnglima Prang, and as he can't hold out he will probably try to escape by the river. Be ready for him, I am going to warn the boats down stream," and turning round the craft disappeared towards the other line of river-sentinels.

No one of course suspected a ruse under such a

bold disguise as that, and, pulling straight for the down-stream boats, steering right on and through them, the Pĕnglima called out, "*Jâga-jâga,* 'be on your guard,' the Shabandar sends orders to watch for the Pĕnglima Prang Sĕmaun, he is trying to escape, I am warning all the boats."

No one could distinctly see who this messenger was, or even catch more than a shadowy glimpse of a spectral craft as she glided through the line, and in the excitement of expectation, the noise of firing and rival battle-shouts on shore, no one took special heed as to which way the messengers went, or whether that was the sound of their oars echoing faintly in the distance.

The Shabandar on his part made no long tarrying, but eager to revenge the murder of his brother, and feeling that at last the Pĕnglima and Haji Ali were in his power, he determined to *mĕng-âmok,* to rush the house at once without waiting for daylight.

Whilst summoning his men for the assault, he heard the cries that told him the besieged were making an attempt to break through his stockades, and without further delay he dashed into Haji Mûsah's house, only to find it empty, the renowned Pĕnglima and his amiable friend gone, and with them a considerable quantity of dollars and every-thing that was both valuable and easily portable.

Torches and an examination of the muddy ground soon established the direction taken, and the missing boat, coupled with the missing property, convinced the least astute that by this way went the Pěnglima Prang Sěmaun.

Many shouted questions from the bank drew forth many assurances from those on the water that no enemy had passed that way. The evidence to the contrary was, however, all too plain, and as the boats one by one came up to the landing-place, and the watchers told their tale, it became evident that once again the Pěnglima Prang Sěmaun had justified his reputation for both daring and resource.

He had made for the sea, his party did not number ten, and they were in one boat. There was still time to overtake or intercept them at the river's mouth, and, as the grey light of dawn began to lift the veil of mist and the freshening breeze swept in chilly gusts over the water, a fleet of boats set off to search the creeks and backwaters, while others had orders to pull straight to the river's mouth, and there take line and see that none passed out to sea.

The Pěnglima meanwhile had wasted no time.

'Twixt the devil behind and the deep sea in front, he had no difficulty in determining which way lay safety ; but he also realised that it could not be an hour, it might be only a few minutes before his ruse would be discovered, and with his crew he could not hope to reach the sea without being overtaken. The rowers needed little exhortation to strain every nerve, and after a few miles had been travelled, the boat was forced through heavy overhanging branches into an all but imperceptible creek, so narrow the entrance and so thoroughly concealed that no one would dream of its existence. The boat could only be got a few yards up this ditch, and the party, leaving it entirely hidden, ensconced themselves in a tangled mass of jungle foliage from which they commanded a view of the river.

Here the fugitives lay all day, and watched the boats of their enemies pass by intent on the fruitless search.

It was not a pleasant place nor did they spend an altogether happy day, for they were not yet out of the wood, indeed the chances of escape were still decidedly against them, but for the moment they were safe, and whatever was to come could not be worse than the situation from which their leader had already extricated them.

Whilst the Pĕnglima was running the gauntlet of the guard-boats his late companions, the men of Lambor, some twenty or thirty in number, were having a worse experience on shore.

Being a large party and in their haste not over-cautious, they were, of course, discovered as they tried to break through the line of stockades. Some were shot, others were speared and *krised* in hand-to-hand encounters, while a few got away to the forest under cover of the darkness. But when these stragglers fully realised that it was a choice between the enemy and painful wandering in a swampy and well-nigh impenetrable jungle, with the prospect of starvation and a lingering death, they chose rather to return to the light and a speedier reckoning.

None of this band returned to Lambor, and if they sought their fate and made an unprovoked attack upon Haji Mûsah it is not altogether sur-prising that to this day there is no wasted affection between the people of Lambor and the Lower Perak Chiefs.

All through that sultry day, as one by one these doomed men appeared from the jungle fastness and went down before the weapons of their adversaries, waiting tirelessly expectant in the certainty that no refuge would be found in those inhospitable depths, the Pĕnglima and his little band lay close in their concealment and longed for sheltering night.

All day long the Shabandar's boats passed hither and thither, and with the nightfall many appeared to abandon the search and returned on the rising tide.

Then an hour or two of the new-born moon, and after that thick darkness.

The Pĕnglima and his friends had regained their boat, and as, about midnight, the tide began to ebb, the vessel was pushed noiselessly out into the river and bracing themselves for a final effort the rowers gripped their oars, stiffened their backs and put their whole strength into the work before them.

The river as it approaches the sea grows wider at every bend, the searchers were exhausted and asleep, or had already returned up-stream, the night was dark and the fugitives were unmolested until, between 4 A.M. and 5 A.M., in the last reach, they saw a line of boats guarding the river's mouth.

There were wide intervals between each vessel, but even in that uncertain light it was impossible for a boat to run this blockade without being seen.

At this final juncture the Pĕnglima's Familiar did not desert him.

Of course the earth ought to have opened and

swallowed up this hardened criminal as it did Korah, Dathan, Abiram, and all their company ; he ought to have been shot or drowned or speared if he were not being reserved for hanging. At any rate this was an excellent opportunity for getting rid of two hardened villains, and a few other passably wicked men. The Lambor people, whose crimes were as snow compared to those of these two arch-criminals, had all met with violent deaths and no miracle, not even so much as a small streak of luck, like falling into a well and being tended by a beautiful maiden, had saved the life of one of them.

Why was it then that, as these cold-blooded assassins cowered together and wondered how they were going to elude the vigilance of their enemies, a palpable miracle was wrought to save their miserable skins ?

It cannot be said that anything very unusual happened, because the thing is of common occurrence, but it was certainly thoughtfully arranged that at that moment there should sail round the bend of the river, in the strongest flow of the ebb-tide (now of course slackening), an enormous mass of floating palms, a very island of foliage broken away from some undermined bank and drifting majestically to the wider waters of the sea.

If these great clumps of root and branch and foliage may be seen sailing every day down a Malay river into the Straits of Malacca, this particular island was so gigantic, that in size at least it was miraculous. It is possible that to another man the passing drift would have suggested nothing, but the Pĕnglima Prang Sĕmaun was on such terms with Fortune that he knew exactly the psychological moment at which to take her. Here he remembered that the Malays call these floating islands *âpong*, and that boats know very much better than to get in their way. His craft then he promptly steered right into the back of this Satan-sent refuge, and, forcing it in amongst the palms and covering it as well as was possible, he calmly sat down and awaited the issue.

The island sailed slowly along, and when the huge mass got near enough to the guard-boats for them to realise their danger, there was a deal of shouting and pulling of anchors, kicking up sleepy boatmen and frantic struggles to avoid this river Juggernaut.

So passed the Pĕnglima Prang Sĕmaun ; not to the vales and Queens of Avilion, but to the open sea, from sore stress to safety, from an earthly death to an earthly life.

One can almost hear him chuckle as he sails

through that last danger and watches his enemies' efforts to get back into their places.

Malays do not pine for manual labour, they had already had more than enough of it, and as they were now being towed idly along, they lay down to sleep, vaguely wondering, in that moment of tired but delicious drowsiness, what occult powers this leader possessed to secure at such a moment the powerful help of this great leviathan, under whose green and shady sails they were being wafted to safety and " the haven where they would be."

A day or two of pleasant coasting, a walk across country, and Pěnglima Prang Sěmaun, with Haji Ali and a considerable booty, arrived safely at Blanja and received the congratulations of his master, the Râja Bendahâra.

We read that when it was the fashion for knights to devote themselves to the service of distressed damsels, they wrought many startling deeds, which cannot always be satisfactorily explained without recognising that devotion in so good a cause was sometimes supernaturally aided.

Unfortunately, the practice has fallen into desuetude ; let us hope it is because the damsels of the nineteenth century are never in distress, want no assistance, or despise that of the mere man.

Malays are perhaps, in some respects, a few hundred years behind the age, and I like to think that in this veracious story the Pĕnglima Prang Sĕmaun made his first appearance as the champion of a lady in distress.

# XIV

# BĔR-HANTU

Striving to reach the mystic source
of things, the secrets of the earth
and sea and air

L. Morris

WE could all see the *tunggul mĕrah*, the crimson streak which boded the death of the King. Looking from the top of our green-terraced hill across the clear wide river late one afternoon, this curious phenomenon appeared in the sky, above the last spur of a picturesque range of mountains which separates the valleys of two considerable streams whose united waters flow into the Straits of Malacca.

Standing on the right bank of the river, a stretch of level land lies between the opposite bank and the foot of this range, and the wealth of foliage hides from view the houses, orchards, and ricefields which cover that fertile plain. But the Sultan's house, a palm-thatched wooden structure, three houses on

147

piles joined together by short platforms after the accepted Malay pattern, stands out clearly enough, rather down-stream than opposite the point of view.

The crimson portent is not visible for long, and we realise that, whatever it means, it is accounted for by the segment of a rainbow shining through a bank of low clouds which obscure the rest of the " arch of heaven," and so blur the prismatic colours that nothing is clearly discernible but a short column of flame, all the more striking for its dull grey background. The tradition of ill-omen is of ancient origin, but the fact that the Sultan now lies grievously ill gives an air of probability to the gossip of the prophets.

That evening, as we sat at dinner, we were suddenly startled by the cry of the banshee. Up till that moment we had none of us had any personal acquaintance with the banshee, but this was it sure enough. A long-drawn-out distressing wail, as of a lost child, repeated at uncertain intervals, now here now there, first on one side of the house and then on the other, at one moment unpleasantly close, and the next a piteous little half-choked sob in the distance. Without any doubt this was the banshee, and as the moonlight was now streaming fitfully through the clouds across the white pillars of the verandah, we thought we might have the good fortune to see this harbinger of doom.

We walked out on to the moonlit terrace, and the beauty of the night was so intense that one felt it as through a new sense.

The hill on which the house stood was cut into a series of terraces, and the highest of these, a wide lawn of velvety grass, was surrounded by tall graceful coco-nut trees, not close together but each standing alone with its spiky leaves clearly delineated against the sky.

Overhead a moon shedding that wonderful soft light only seen in the East, where atmosphere, foliage, and all the surroundings seem specially designed to make the ascendancy of the Queen of Night superbly beautiful.

The exquisite feathery fronds of the bamboo, bending in graceful curves, with each leaf clearly defined against a background of grey-blue sky ; a dozen varieties of palms, from the lofty coco-nut and the stately jagary to the thick clumps of *bertam*, like gigantic ferns ; picturesque groups of flowering trees and shrubs on terrace after terrace, carry the eye down to the shimmering gleam of the wide river on which the moonlight falls lovingly, throwing into greater contrast the deep shadows that lie under the overhanging foliage of the banks. Four miles of glistening water, then the river narrows and fades into the mist-enshrouded forest.

Close beneath us twinkle the lights of the village, the houses spreading from river-brink to the high ground which rises abruptly on our left. In front and on either side, range after range of jungle-covered hills, from fifteen hundred to several thousands of feet in height. There is a luminous haze over all distant objects, giving the idea of indefinite height and distance, making all things vague and unsubstantial, yet infinitely satisfying that other sense which only awakes under the influence of perfect beauty.

The extraordinary charm of this scene intoxicated us as with draughts of nectar, and in that enravishment kings, omens, and ghostly warnings were forgotten.

But hark! Yes, there is the cry, wailing in the distance—now much nearer, and now—before our very eyes the banshee itself!

Sailing slowly through the air between the feathery leaves of the palms, like a lost soul wending its uncertain, purposeless way through the balmy Eastern night, was a creature with heavy dark wings, a head disproportionately large, and horns, veritable horns! As it slowly passed and moaned its childlike plaint, no reasonable being could doubt that he had heard and seen the messenger of death.

That weird apparition, sobbing its fateful cry, broke the spell under which we had stood enthralled, and though we felt that the King's fate was sealed, that did not prevent us from returning to dinner.

Just after midnight a scared Malay came to say that it was feared the Sultan was dying. I hurried down the hill, took boat across the river, and, stumbling along the bank, reached the house where the sick man lay.

I entered upon a peculiar scene. I said the building was in three parts, the first a sort of anteroom, beyond which strangers of inferior rank did not in ordinary circumstances pass; then came the principal structure, which consisted of one large room, wooden pillars dividing off verandahs on either side, while the third house was exclusively devoted to women, and attached to it was an excrescence forming the kitchen.

The unsteady light of several lamps and many candles showed that both the centre and ante-rooms were full of people sitting on the mats which covered the floor. There must have been between one and two hundred present, and I noticed that there were about equal numbers of men and women, and all the principal Malays of the neighbourhood were there. The curtains which usually divided the centre room were up, but on one side there was evidently a bed, screened by patchwork hangings, and there I concluded His Highness lay.

It was plain from the preparations that, despairing of effecting a cure by native medicines administered by native doctors, it was intended to try a little witchcraft and have a performance of what is called *Bĕr-hantu*. That seemed to me to fall in very well with the *tunggul mêrah* and the banshee, and I was therefore quite prepared for the raising of the Devil or any other uncanny manifestation.

I may as well say here that *hantu* is a ghost, devil or spirit, and *bĕr-hantu* means *to devil*, to raise the devil, or, at any rate, to engage in something as nearly akin to a witches' revel on the Brocken as Malay traditions and surroundings will permit. It is a treatment commonly resorted to in Perak when other remedies fail. When, however, the friends of the patient decide that the time has arrived for *bĕr-hantu*, nothing will satisfy them but to have it, and if the sick man or woman dies during the performance, there is still the satisfaction of knowing that everything was done for them which love and skill could devise, and the issue was with God. *La-illahâ il-Allah, Muhammad Rasul-Allah*—" There is but one God, and Muhammad is His Prophet."

This pious confession of faith has, however, nothing to do with the *bĕr-hantu;* it comes in afterwards when the seal of death is so evidently on the lips of the sufferer that his friends cease to call on the Devil, and commend the soul of the dying man to God. The *bĕr-hantu* is, of course, a survival of præ-Islam darkness, and the priests abominate it, or say they do ; but they have to be a little careful, because the highest society affects the practice of the Black Art.

To return to the King's house. In the middle of the floor was spread a *puâdal*, a small narrow mat, at one end of which was seated a middle-aged woman dressed like a man in a short-sleeved jacket, trousers, a *sârong*, and a scarf fastened tightly round her waist. At the other end of the mat was a large newly-lighted candle in a candlestick. Between the woman and the taper were two or three small vessels containing rice coloured with turmeric, parched *padi*, and perfumed water. An attendant sat near at hand.

The woman in male attire was the *Pâwang*, the Raiser of Spirits, the Witch, not of Endor, but of as great repute in her own country and among her own people. In ordinary life she was an amusing lady named Raja Ngah, a scion of the reigning house on the female side and a member of a family skilled in all matters pertaining to occultism. In a corner of the room were five or six girls holding native drums, instruments with a skin stretched over one side only, and this is beaten usually with the fingers. The leader of this orchestra was the daughter of Raja Ngah.

Shortly after I sat down, the proceedings began by the *Pâwang* covering her head and face with a silken cloth, while the orchestra began to sing a weird melody in an unknown tongue. I was told it was the spirit language ; the air was one specially pleasing to a particular *Jin*, or Spirit, and the invocation, after reciting his praises, besought him to come from the mountains or the sea, from underground or overhead, and relieve the torments of the King.

As the song continued, accompanied by the rhythmical beating of the drums, the *Pâwang* sat with shrouded head in front of the lighted taper, holding in her right hand against her left breast a

small sheaf of the grass called *daun sambau* tied
tightly together and cut square at top and bottom.

This *châdak* she shook, together with her whole
body, by a stiffening of the muscles, while all eyes
were fixed upon the taper.

At first the flame was steady, but by and by, as
the singers screamed more loudly to attract the
attention of the laggard Spirit, the wick began to
quiver and flare up, and it was manifest to the
initiated that the *Jin* was introducing himself into
the candle. By some means the *Pâwang*, who was
now supposed to be "possessed" and no longer
conscious of her actions, became aware of this, and
she made obeisance to the taper, sprinkling the
floor round it with saffron-coloured rice and perfumed water; then, rising to her feet and followed
by the attendant, she performed the same ceremony
before each male member of the reigning family
present in the room, murmuring all the while a
string of gibberish addressed to the Spirit. This
done, she resumed her seat on the mat, and, after a
brief pause, the minstrels struck up a different air,
and, singing the praises of another *Jin*, called upon
him to come and relieve the King's distress.

I ascertained that each Malay State has its own
special Spirits, each district is equally well provided,

and there are even some to spare for special individuals. In this particular State there are four principal *Jin;* they are the *Jin ka-râja-an,* the State
Spirit—also called *Junjong dŭnia udâra*—Supporter
of the Firmament ; *Mâia udâra,* the Spirit of the
Air ; *Mahkôta si- râja Jin,* the Crown of Royal
Spirits ; and *S'tan Ali.*

These four are known as *Jin âruah,* Exalted
Spirits, and they are the guardians of the Sultan
and the State. As one star exceeds another in
glory, so one *Jin* surpasses another in renown, and
I have named them in the order of their greatness.
In their honour four white and crimson umbrellas
were hung in the room, presumably for their use
when they arrived from their distant homes. Only
the Sultan of the State is entitled to traffic with
these distinguished Spirits ; when summoned they
decline to move unless appealed to with their own
special invocations, set to their own peculiar music,
sung by at least four singers and led by a *Bĕduan*
(singer) of the royal family. The *Jin ka-râja-an* is
entitled to have the royal drums played by the State
drummers if his presence is required, but the other
three have to be satisfied with the instruments I
have described.

There are common devils who look after common

people : such as *Hantu Songkei, Hantu Malâyu and Hantu Blîan;* the last the " Tiger Devil," but out of politeness he is called " Blîan," to save his feelings.

Then there is *Kĕmâla ajâib,* the " Wonderful Jewel," *Israng,* Raja Ngah's special familiar, and a host of others. Most *hantu* have their own special *Pâwangs,* and several of these were carrying on similar proceedings in adjoining buildings, in order that the sick monarch might reap all the benefits to be derived from a consultation of experts, and, as one spirit after another notified his advent by the upstarting flame of the taper, it was impossible not to feel that one was getting into the very best society.

Meanwhile a sixteen-sided stand, about six inches high and shaped like this diagram, had been placed on the floor near the *Pâwang's* mat. The stand was decorated with yellow cloth ; in its centre stood an enormous candle, while round it were gaily decorated rice and toothsome delicacies specially prized by *Jin.* There was just room to sit on this stand, which is called *Pĕtrâna panchalôgam* (meaning a seat of this par-

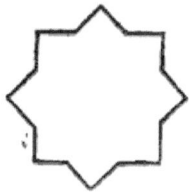

ticular shape), and the Sultan, supported by many attendants, was brought out and sat upon it. A veil was placed on his head, the various vessels were put in his hands, he spread the rice round the taper, sprinkled the perfume, and having received into his hand an enormous *châdak* of grass, calmly awaited the coming of the *Jin Ka-râja-an*, while the minstrels shouted for him with all their might.

The Sultan sat there for some time, occasionally giving a convulsive shudder, and when this taper had duly flared up and all the rites had been performed, His Highness was conducted back again to his couch, and the *Pâwang* continued her ministrations alone.

Whilst striding across the floor, she suddenly fell down as though shot, and it was explained to me that Israng, the spirit by whom she was possessed, had seen a dish-cover, and that the sight always frightened him to such an extent that his *Pâwang* fell down. The cause of offence was removed, and the performance continued.

There are other spirits who cannot bear the barking of a dog, the mewing of a cat, and so on.

Just before dawn there was a sudden confusion within the curtains which hid the Sultan's couch ; they were thrown aside, and there lay the King, to all appearance in a swoon. The *Jin Ka-râja-an* had taken possession of the sick body, and the mind was no longer under its owner's control.

For a little while there was great excitement, and then the King recovered consciousness, was carried to a side verandah and a quantity of cold water poured over him.

So ended the *séance*.

Shortly after, the Sultan, clothed and in his right mind, sent to say he would like to speak to me. He told me he took part in this ceremony to please his people and because it was a very old custom, and he added, "I did not know you were there till just now ; I could not see you because I was not myself and did not know what I was doing."

The King did not die, after all—on the contrary, I was sent for twice again because he was not expected to live till the morning, and yet he cheated Death—for a time.

That reminds me of the banshee. I saw it sitting in a Malay house some months later, and they told me the boys had caught it, that it was an owl, and its name was *Toh ka-tampi*. It had very round, yellow eyes, and there was no mistake about the horns. It seems that with Malays it is an ill-omened bird, the herald of misfortune and death, and it shares this reputation with two other owls, which are called respectively *Tumbok lârong*, that is "Nail the coffin," and *Chârek kafan*, "Rend the cloth for the shroud." *Toh ka-tampi* means "Old-man-winnow-the-rice-for-the-burial-feast." The names are rather gruesome, and are said to be suggested by the peculiar cries of these "ghost birds."

# XV

# THE KING'S WAY

We know what Heaven or Hell may
bring
But no man knoweth the mind of
the King
RUDYARD KIPLING

H E was the Sultan of an important Malay State, but to those who knew him best he was, and will remain, "Craddock's King," principally because he always sent for Craddock whenever he wanted anything that he thought needed the assistance of a European officer, and, on the rare occasions when he travelled outside his own dominions, Craddock used to go with him as guide, interpreter, and shield.

The King was one with whom things had gone badly until the appearance of the white man in his country. His character had not endeared him to the people, who should have been his subjects, but were, almost without exception, his enemies ; and the consequence was that when he ought to have been elected to a high office, and later, when his birth entitled him to be nominated Sultan, his claims were ignored in favour of junior men. Up to the age of fifty or more he had passed his life in poverty, and even in want, and often in open resistance to such authority as existed. These strained relations with his own people made him loyal to the British, and as his claims were indisputable, and the opportunity came when they might be satisfied, he at last attained to the position which was his by right.

I will try to draw the man as he was at this time. Tall for a Malay, rather fair, with grey hair and a white moustache ; very broad-shouldered and thick-set, a powerful figure, though now inclined to over-stoutness ; a firm, upright carriage ; in his face an exceeding *hauteur*, and in his manner something more than this—the plain evidence of a masterful and overbearing disposition. The strength of mind, the obstinacy of character, were writ large in both face and figure ; while an imperious manner was accentuated by a loud voice and impatient speech, caused to some extent by the difficulty of understanding one whose teeth were few, and whose tongue was plainly over-large.

The King affected gay colours, and his appearance, when he took his walks abroad, was striking, not to say remarkable. A tartan silk jacket, combining many violent colours and fastened at the neck only, clothed his body; this jacket had a high collar which enclosed the wearer's bull-neck and reached to the ears. The nether garment was a pair of very wide and loose white silk trousers fastened by many yards of a scarlet silk waist-cloth. These trousers reached a point low down on the calf of the leg, leaving a fair expanse of uncovered limb between them and the sky-blue canvas shoes which encased the stockingless feet. On his head, tilted rakishly over one ear, the King wore a wonderful round bright yellow cap, flat on the top with stiff sides, on which were sewn, in Arabic characters of black cloth, a verse from the Korân.

In his waist-cloth the King usually carried a short knife in a polished wooden sheath, and when walking he leant upon a spear or long bamboo stick. Both hands and feet were white with an unnatural and mottled whiteness, caused, His Highness averred, by eating the flesh of the white buffalo, and, in walking, the toes were turned out to such an extent as to give a decided waddle.

For people with whom loyalty to their rajas is an article of faith, the dislike in which the King was held by them was extraordinary. It is charitable to suppose that early disappointment had embittered his life, for he possessed good qualities. He was undeniably intelligent, and had a wider knowledge of his country and its ancient customs than any other man in it. He knew his own mind, was determined to obstinacy, and asked counsel of few. He was a keen sportsman, courageous, and, having sought the friendship of the British, never wavered in his loyalty. If it be said that in this he consulted his own interest and knew his unpopularity with his own people, his consistency and good faith were still a merit. On the other hand, his defects and vices were numerous, and just those likely to earn him the dislike of Malays. He was incredibly mean, he was overbearing to cruelty, rapaciously grasping, jealous of the good fortune of any of his subjects, selfish, difficult of access, and unconcerned with the misfortunes of others ; vindictive to those who offended him or opposed his wishes, a gambler who nearly always contrived to win, and in matters where the other sex were concerned, decidedly unreliable. He was not an opium-smoker, nor was he in any sense a religious man, and, though the "Defender of the Faith" in his own country, he observed none of its outward forms. It cannot, therefore, be said that he was in good odour with the priesthood and yet one of his firmest friends —for a time—was the priest of the neighbouring village who, whenever a witness was needed to support the King in any action or statement, was ready both to vouch to supposed facts and prove his master's case by the authority of Muhammadan writings.

The constant appeal to the priest for justification and the persistence with which this man found excellent reasons for the King's peculiar methods was a little discouraging; but there came an estrangement. The King, accompanied by the priest and others, visited a neighbouring British possession, stayed there some days, and at the moment of his return was faced by a serious indignity. It appeared that someone in this place who did not understand the King's peculiarities had, or thought he had, sold to His Highness a tricycle and a musical-box for which he could not obtain payment, and, having ascertained that the King was going and did not care about the things, this misguided individual somehow obtained a summons against His Highness to appear before a local tribunal and answer to the plaint.

The King, being informed, expressed his extreme unconcern, and said that, as it was the priest's business and his only, he could settle it. The priest raised the amount necessary to meet the bill, and the party returned to their own State with the musical-box and tricycle.

Then "a private pique arose" between King and Priest as to who should finally pay for these playthings. For the first time these firm friends appeared in opposition to each other, and both parties gave their respective versions of the transaction before a highly edified and delighted Council of Arbitration.

First the King : He knew nothing of any musical-box, did not like musical-boxes, had no ear for music, and did not understand the discordant noises made by these inventions of the white man. He had seen a thing of the kind in his house, had heard it, had even himself made it play its absurd tunes, did not enjoy it in the least, and had done it without thinking, but knew it would please the priest as he had bought the thing, and he supposed he would not have done so unless he wanted to have it played.

As for the tricycle, how in the name of misfortune could a tricycle concern him ? The bare idea of a

man of his age and figure riding a tricycle was
enough to make a dog bark (and here His Highness
laughed consumedly at the spectacle he had con-
jured up). Had anyone ever seen him ride a
tricycle? Where was he going to ride it? Was
it on the sandy shore of the river where he lived?
and if not there, then where? He understood that
tricycles would neither go through the jungle nor
across *padi* fields, and, if he were to take "the
creature" out shooting, he supposed it would not
greatly help him to get a shot at a bison or a
rhinoceros. Did anyone imagine he was going to
carry letters? that he was going to join the Post
Office? If the imputation were not so stupid he
could almost be angry with the priest, a man whom
he had heard over and over again say that the one
thing he desired was a tricycle, something on which
he could take exercise, and at the same time get
about his district. He had even asked him, the
King, to lend him money to buy the machine, but
he had no money to lend and tried to dissuade the
man because he thought that in his inexperience he
might fall and hurt himself. Malays did not understand things that ran on three wheels without ever
a horse or a bullock, or even a buffalo to pull them.
He saw the tricycle lying under his house, and he

heard the priest haggling with someone about the price, but he would take any oath that the priest or anyone else could devise that he had never set eyes on the man who sold the thing. All he knew was that he had been insulted by the issue of a summons because of the priest's extravagant tastes, and, while any one who liked might pay, it would not be he.

Then the Priest :

Long before they left the State, His Highness told him that when they made this visit it was his desire to purchase a musical-box (in the sweet strains of which his soul delighted) and a tricycle, the beautiful three-wheeled silent carriage which cost little to start with and nothing to keep, wanted no horses, nor harness, nor expensive and impertinent horse-keepers, which never shied at bullock-carts or ran away from elephants, and which lasted through the lives of many beasts. Therefore, he, the priest, the obedient slave of the King, had sought the sweet-voiced box and the stomachless carriage, and after much difficulty he had found them. By the express order of the King the priest had bidden the owners bring them to the house in which the King was lodging, and there the whole details of the two transactions were arranged.

The people who trafficked in these goods could not
be taken into the presence of his master, and, indeed, the King had expressly declined to see them
(was not the King all-wise?), but they had been
brought into a room of the house across which
hung a heavy curtain, and while he, the priest, discussed the terms with the seller on one side, the
King sat on the other, and not only heard all that
was said, but in the end, when the priest went
behind the curtain to consult his royal master, had
expressed his entire approval of the price, only
stipulating that he should first hear the box sing
and ride the stomachless horse. This he had
arranged with some little difficulty, because the
sellers were needy men and wanted the money;
moreover, they seemed to distrust his master, the
King, for some reason which he could not fathom.
But he arranged that the singing-box and the seat
on three wheels should stay with his master for four
days, and that then they should be returned or paid
for; those were the orders of the King. So they
stayed, and the King turned the handle of the box
and made it sing, or, more often, from prayer-time
to prayer-time he, the priest, had to turn the handle
and make music, and the King drank in the sound
and was glad. As for the three wheels, they ay

under the house, and the King looked upon the machine and said it was good and cheap and would eat nothing.

These are the words of the Priest : "The four days went by and the men came to be paid, and I told my master, but he seemed to be busy with other things, and I sent them away to come again the next day. In this way the time passed till the day for our departure, and I knew the men who owned the box and the carriage were angry, but I saw my master wanted the things. When at last the trouble came, and the King said it was not his business but mine, I told the men they could take the box and the carriage back because they did not please the King, but they would not, and I was afraid lest shame should come on my master, and I went out and borrowed the money and paid it. Could I, who am a priest, play with a box that sings not of God nor the Prophet ? Can I, who am a poor man, who only live to pray and to preach, to exhort the living and to bury the dead, can I ride on the stomachless horse with three wheels, I whose duty is in the mosque and by the grave ? My master the King knows that in this thing as in others I have but obeyed the voice of my master."

So Church and State quarrelled, and the priest

found no more favour in the sight of the King. But there were many who said:

> "*Sĕpĕrti Nasrûan dĕngan Bahtek*
> *Bĕr-sâtu rangkêsa*
> *Bĕr-chĕrei jâdi sentôsa.*"

"They are like Râja Nasrûan and his minister Bahtek; their union brought ruin, their divorce solace." Indeed, it was the opportunity of the proverb-monger, and such sayings as, "It is sometimes one's own forefinger which pokes one in the eye," and, "While you carry the Râja's business on your head, don't forget to keep your own under your arm," were heard on all sides.

The King had a clerk who had served him faithfully for twenty years or more. The clerk had a wife, and the King's eye fell upon her approvingly; so the King sent the clerk into a far country to chase a wild bird, and bestowed his favour upon the wife who remained under his care. The King also bestowed upon the lady sundry jewels of price, things that please poor heathen women with hardly any moral character and no education to speak of.

By-and-by the King got tired of the woman, as unprincipled Eastern kings will do, and he sought about for some means, not to rid himself of her, that was simple enough, but to get back his gifts (for they would serve again as they had done already) and at the same time to throw a little dust in the eyes of the clerk, who was known to be on his way back. Accordingly, a youth of no account was arrested by the King's people, and charged with carrying on a *liaison* with the lady during the absence of her husband. The crime was, of course, aggravated by the fact that she was under the special protection of the King! The clear proof of guilt was the alleged possession by the woman of a *sârong*\* belonging to the man.

This charge was sufficient ground for the display of royal displeasure, and procured the restitution of the jewels, but it failed to convince anyone that the man accused by the King had done any wrong, and, in spite of the strenuous exertions of His Highness to get the man banished from the country, nothing was done to him. The plan, therefore, miscarried to some extent, and when the clerk returned it is probable that he learnt the facts, for he declined to further serve the King, and even said bluntly things about his late master that were not altogether loyal.

I have elsewhere stated that Malays try to wipe

---

\* The *Sârong* is the Malay national garment, a sort of skirt, usually in tartan, worn by men and women alike.

out, what in their uncivilised minds they count as dishonour, in a savage and bloodthirsty fashion, but this does not apply when the offender is a raja and the injured man of lesser rank. The person of a raja is sacred to a Malay, and if he feels that he has been disgraced beyond bearing, the result will probably be, sooner or later, an access of blind fury resulting in a case of *âmok*.

The King had as many wives as the Muhammadan law permitted, and, as his country possessed the infinite blessing of a civil list which limited his own income, he was always anxious that whenever he took to himself a new wife she should receive an allowance from the State. His Highness made a special point of this grant to the ladies, because he said the knowledge that if they divorced him or compelled him to divorce them they would lose the allowance, had an excellent effect on their behaviour. He had succeeded in securing allowances for several wives, when a new lady, named Raja Sarefa, consented to share the royal smiles, and the King immediately applied on her behalf for the usual civil list. The application, however, was not successful, though several times renewed.

Then the King fell ill of some fell disease that no native medicine-man could diagnose, and the evil spirit, with which he seemed to be troubled, had its will of him, so that all men said the King must die.

During an interval of temporary return to consciousness, when for a few hours the patient seemed to have a rest from the attacks of the tormentor, he ordered that a young nephew should be sent for, also a divorced wife of his own, and a priest. Then, against the earnest wishes of both parties, he insisted upon these young people being married in his presence, and shortly after relapsed into his former state.

After weeks of torment, when every day seemed certain to be his last, the iron constitution prevailed, and the King recovered. In the first days of his convalescence I went to see him, and found him lying on his bed, in his eyes the light of consciousness and intelligence, and sitting by him the wife, Raja Sarefa.

He was weak, spoke slowly and in a small voice, but said that by God's grace he only wanted time to regain his strength. After expressing my thankfulness at seeing him so well on the way to recovery, I said that I had often been over to see him when he was ill, and that the Raja Sarefa had tended him with extraordinary devotion, never seeming to leave his bedside. At once he said, "You noticed that, did you?" I replied that I had been very much struck by her care of him. "I was blind," he said; "I do not know what happened, but I am very glad you remarked how carefully Sarefa nursed me, and that you have mentioned it, for now you will recognise that she ought to have an allowance."

In the presence of the lady, even though she did not raise her eyes from the floor, it was difficult not to recognise that, if curses come home to roost, blessings sometimes go astray.

After a respite of eighteen months, the evil spirit again took possession of the King, and this time made short work of him.

The scientific explanation, deriding the evil-spirit theory, said that a tumour on the brain, caused by no matter what, accounted for the first attack, and that as sometimes, but rarely, happens, the growth was for a time arrested, the tumour contracted, and the pressure on the brain was removed. But the mischief was there, and a sudden rapid development of the disease brought on a return of the symptoms, a violent but hopeless struggle, and death.

It is the custom in the country of which I now write to, in a manner, canonise its Sultans. At the burial, when the moment arrives for carrying the body to the place of sepulture, the dead man is given a new name, by which he is ever afterwards known. That name is chosen with some reference to his earthly life. Thus, there is Al-mĕrhum or Mĕrhum Pâsir Panjang (that is, "The Sultan who died at Pâsir Panjang"), Mĕrhum Kahar-Allah ("The late Sultan to whom God gave strength"), and so on.

When this King was buried, the name conferred upon him was Mĕrhum Rafir-Allah, and the meaning is, "May God pardon him."

NOTE.—Since writing the above, I have read the following in the *Home News*:

"In the Lord Mayor's Court on Oct. 14, before the Assistant Judge and a jury, the case of 'Fischer *v.* Brown' was concluded. This (says the *Times*) was an action brought by Fischer and Co., a firm of Bombay merchants, to recover from Messrs. Brown, Saville, and Co., who carry on business in this country, the sum of £73, money paid by the plaintiffs to the defendants, for which they had received no consideration. It appeared that in July, 1892, the plaintiffs received an order for a special perambulator, which was to be given to His Highness

Tikah Sahib, Rajah of Patalia, as a birthday present
by his secretary, Sham Shir Sing.   The perambulator was to be painted dark green and old gold,
which were the colours of the Rajah, and there was
to be a good strong musical-box under the seat, and
also an automatic arrangement by which the perambulator, on being wound up, would run by itself.
This order was given to the defendants by the
plaintiffs on July 4, and the perambulator was to
be ready for shipment to Bombay by Aug. 15, in
order that it should reach the Rajah by Oct. 1,
which was the date of his birthday.   The defendants
did not finish the work in time, and the Rajah's
birthday had passed before the present arrived, and
then the secretary refused to take it, and it had to
be sent back.   In the meantime the defendants had
drawn a bill upon the plaintiffs for the price of the
perambulator, and this the plaintiffs had accepted
and had paid the money, which they were now
suing to recover.   For the defence it was stated
that the cause of the delay in delivering the perambulator was Mr. F. Fischer's interference.   The
wheels and springs of the perambulator, it had
been agreed, should be electro-plated, but when
Mr. Fischer heard this he said it would not suit the
Rajah, and they must be gilded.   He was told this

could not be done in time, and it was implied by
the orders he gave (which were that the perambulator should have elephant-headed handles and
papier-maché figures of elephants and peacocks)
that a further allowance of time would be given.
The jury found a verdict for the plaintiffs for the
amount claimed."

# XVI

# A MALAY ROMANCE

Every heart in which heaven has set
the lamp of love, whether that heart
inclines to Mosque or Synagogue, if
its name be written in the Book of
Love it is freed from the fear of Hell,
and the hope of Paradise

JUSTIN McCARTHY's *Omar
Khayyam*

A QUARTER of a century ago there lived on the bank of a broad river, just at the point where stream meets tide, a Malay Raja and his youthful wife. She has been dead for twenty years, but in this land of brief regrets her memory is still green, the fame of her wit and beauty has become a byword with the people.

She was a girl of royal descent; her name, Raja Maimûnah. Exceeding fair, for a Malay, slight but graceful in figure, with very small hands and feet, an oval face and splendid eyes, glistening blue-white wells in which floated, lotus-like, the dark iris, flashing or wooing in changeful expression

from wide-open or half-closed lids deeply shaded by
long black lashes. Her nose was small, straight,
and well cut, and the curved smiling lips disclosed
teeth of perfect shape and singular whiteness. In
either cheek a dimple, *lĕsong mâti*, as the Malays
call it, the dimple which so fascinates the beholder
that it will lure him even unto death. Her jet-
black hair, fringing the forehead in an oval frame,
was drawn straight back over the well-shaped head
and fastened in a simple knot with four ruby-studded
hairpins ; the heads firmly fixed against one side of
the coil, while the golden points protruded for an
inch or more beyond the other.

Her dress was that worn by all ladies of rank,
and usually consisted of a silk skirt of softly-
blended colours reaching to the ankles and fastened
at the waist by a belt with a large golden buckle.
The only other garment was a satin jacket of some
dark colour on which were stitched cunningly-
wrought designs of beaten gold. This jacket had
a tight collar, and the close-fitting sleeves were
fastened by a long row of jewelled buttons reaching
almost from wrist to elbow ; it was loose at the
waist and just covered the belt. Tiny heelless
shoes, embroidered with gold and silver thread,
completed the attire.

When out of doors, the Raja Maimûnah would wear a veil of darkest blue, black or white gossamer embroidered with very narrow gold ribbon, a most becoming head-dress, the product of Arabian skill. Over this, again, was held coquettishly, to conceal the face from male eyes, a scarf of rich Malay-red silk, heavy with interwoven threads of gold, while one or two more silken *sârongs* of varying colour and richness of material were worn over the under-skirt.

Jewels depend upon the wealth and station of the wearer, but Maimûnah's jacket was fastened with buttons that matched the hairpins. She was seldom seen without diamond solitaires in the ears and a number of diamond rings on her fingers, while on State occasions she wore heavy gold bangles on her wrists and one or more gold neck-laces.

I cannot draw an equally attractive picture of Raja Iskander, the husband of this lady. He was about thirty years of age, while she was one-and-twenty. He was short and spare for a Malay, and his distinguishing features were a large ugly mouth with a downward turn at the corners and an almost perpetual expression of extreme discontent.

His vanity was inordinate, his extravagance

continually led him into difficulty, and he smoked opium to excess and to the neglect of all his duties and his interests ; moreover, he lacked courage, and sought counsel from men of no standing, whose only thought was their own profit.

A Malay Raja has many wives. He begins early and rings the changes often, until (especially if he have pretensions to become ultimately the ruler of his country, as was the case with Iskander) his relatives decide that he should marry a lady of his own rank. Then, if he is young, her people usually insist that any wife he has must be divorced, and, that done, the marriage takes place.

At the time of which I write, Raja Iskander had been married to Maimûnah for about three years ; she was the mother of two children, but her husband thought he had good reason to doubt her fidelity, and he was palpably neglecting her for a concubine. That he should have other wives or concubines was of course only what she had been educated to expect, and, in acting on his right, Raja Iskander was simply following the practice of his ancestors and the custom of the country. The Muhammadan law is nevertheless extremely strict in its injunctions that all wives are to be treated with equal consideration, and, while their claims are clear, the concubine has none. To neglect a wife for a concubine is a dire offence to Malay women, and the slight is enormously exaggerated when the wife is of high birth, and the favourite only a woman of the people.

The house where Raja Iskander then lived was within a hundred feet of the bank of the stream, an unattractive spot fifty miles from the mouth of the river, but yet not far enough to escape the tidal influence and the unlovely accompaniments of turbid water, muddy banks, and flat surroundings. Raja Iskander passed a good deal of his time in boats, the lazy life suited him and his habits, and, instead of having to provide a house for each of the ladies in his harem, he supplied a boat. That was much more economical, and economy was an object, for, like many people with extravagant tastes, his extravagance was purely selfish.

The boats lay in the river in front of the house, and as Raja Iskander's presence was the excuse for a rendezvous of all the gamblers, cock-fighters, and opium-smokers of the neighbourhood, a good many boats besides his own were always in attendance.

Amongst the visitors attracted to this spot at this time was a man called Raja Slêman, a stranger from a neighbouring State.

It might have been the cock-fighting or the gambling always to be found in the society of Raja Iskander that drew Raja Slêman to the place. It might also have been the congenial society of another opium-smoker, or possibly the fame of Raja Maimûnah's attractions. Whatever the lodestone, Raja Slêman appeared with two boats and about fifteen followers, and, once arrived, he elected to remain.

Raja Iskander passed most of his time on the water, but Maimûnah lived in the house on shore. A very modest dwelling it was ; a building of mat sides and thatched roof raised from the damp and muddy earth on wooden piles, a flight of steps led into the front of the house and a ladder served for exit at the back. The interior accommodation consisted of a closed-in verandah, one large room, and a kitchen tacked on behind.

The edges of the muddy river were fringed by the *nipah* palm, which is never seen beyond tidal influences ; the banks were covered by rank grasses, the country was flat and desolate, the jungle insignificant, and in the heat of the day the oppression of steaming mud and shelterless plain was so great that sleep seemed to force itself on insect, reptile, and every living thing.

At night the myriads of fireflies sparkling in the riverside bushes, their twinkling lights reflected in the water, gave some relief to tired eyes ; but the gain in the change of temperature and scene was hardly appreciated when the mosquitoes and sand-flies began their merciless attacks.

Under such circumstances and amidst such surroundings, Raja Slêman came into the life of Maimûnah.

He was about the same age as Raja Iskander, but in other respects there was a striking difference between the two men. Slêman was a man of pleasing features, extremely quiet, and of courtly manners ; the casual observer would probably fail to realise that this outward appearance concealed a firm determination and a dauntless courage. Of worldly goods he had little enough, and small prospect of multiplying them, but in rank he was almost, if not quite, the equal of Raja Iskander.

One day as Slêman sat in his boat he saw Maimûnah and her maidens come down to the river to bathe. In his country he had never beheld a woman as beautiful as this one, and he fell hope-lessly in love with Iskander's wife. Then each day he watched for her, and never failed, morning and evening, to follow her with his eyes for the few moments when she slowly wended her way from house to river and back again.

Meanwhile, Maimûnah, suffering from the *spretæ injuria formæ* and chafing under the monotony of existence, had heard all about the arrival of Slêman and readily listened to the tales of his valorous deeds. Soon she began to look for him, and as he was ever watching for her coming it was not long before their eyes met. He pleased her, and, when she saw in his face the admiration he had no desire to conceal, she would drop the covering that hid all but her eyes, and what he then beheld only increased his passion.

Malay ladies are adepts in speaking the language of the eyes, the chances of verbal speech are but few, and so carefully is this art cultivated, so thoroughly understood, that principals and witnesses never fail to rightly interpret the signs.

Slêman and Maimûnah had already mutually declared themselves without the exchange of a syllable, and it was with perfect confidence that Slêman sought a closer intimacy by the friendly aid of a messenger.

Iskander was too much engaged with his opium and his latest favourite, too generally satisfied with himself, to notice what was going on. Had he realised the state of affairs he would not have been indifferent to the disgrace that must be his, should his wife's *liaison* become public property. It is unlikely that he had any suspicion of Slêman, but, if he had, it would never occur to him that any man would have the courage to do more than carry on a clandestine intrigue, and of that he suspected Maimûnah had already been guilty. Least of all would it seem possible for a foreigner supported by a dozen followers to brave the power and resentment of well nigh the greatest chief of a powerful State.

In this, however, he was misled by the *suave* manners of the quiet stranger.

Slêman's suit prospered, and he was not satisfied to continue indefinitely filling the *rôle* of false friend to Iskander and fearful lover to his wife. However much he despised the man, however easily he found he could profit by Iskander's indifference, he meant to play a bolder game and make Maimûnah his own at all hazards if she were prepared to face the risk.

Her courage was equal to his own (for failure meant probably death to her as to him), and one night, while Iskander lay in his boat dreaming over his opium-pipe, the stranger was carrying off his royal spouse within earshot, almost from under his very eyes.

Once in Slêman's boat, and the bark had been silently unmoored and allowed to drift out of sight and hearing, little time was lost in getting out the oars and pulling with might and main down river towards the coast.

All night long the rowers bent to their work, but when morning broke and less than half the distance to the river's mouth had been traversed, Slêman ordered the men to pull in to the bank, fasten up the boat and rest.

It seemed a foolhardy proceeding to waste the precious time, for with the dawn the elopement would be discovered and Iskander would be in pursuit before the sun had cleared the tops of the jungle trees.

Raja Slêman's quiet serenity was not disturbed by anticipations of capture or fear of the outraged husband's fury. On the contrary, he procured a small boat and a messenger, and he indited a letter to Raja Iskander, informing him he had carried away the Raja Maimûnah, but that he had not gone far, having only reached the place he named. He added that he would wait there for one night and one day against the coming of any who might wish to try and take the lady from him, and that after that time he should continue his journey to the coast and thence to his own country.

Raja Iskander received this missive whilst yet undecided what course to take in the untoward disaster that had befallen him. The letter did not greatly help him to arrive at a decision, and he was still discussing with his chiefs who should have the honour of pursuing and punishing the abductor when the twenty-four hours expired.

Neither Iskander nor any of his people ever started on that quest, and Raja Slêman carried Maimûnah in safety to his own country.

The disconsolate husband, whose ideas were in accord with a civilisation beyond the education or sympathetic comprehension of his subjects, decided to divorce his faithless wife and leave her lover to marriage and the punishment of his own conscience. It is a painful fact that this conduct earned him not the admiration but the contempt of his people.

Iskander had one revenge : he discovered amongst Maimûnah's women two who had carried messages between the lovers. One was a woman of twenty-five, the other a girl of fourteen, and both were incontinently strangled.

As for Slêman and Maimûnah, they were duly married, and she bore him a daughter in all respects like her mother, though not, the old people say, her peer in beauty. The *laudator temporis acti* is a common and flourishing plant in Malâya.

In the two children born before the elopement, it is difficult to trace any resemblance to their mother.

Maimûnah died years and years ago, the victim of a malignant disease ; but Slêman still lives in his own country, his hair is getting grey, but otherwise he shows few signs of age. Time has only intensified the courteous bearing and quiet repose of manner which seem to fitly accompany his gentle winning voice ; no one would suspect that this man, almost single-handed, carried off the chief spouse of an Oriental prince, and then defied the whole country to take her from him.

There are no local bards to record Slêman's story in deathless song, and the people are so impregnated with vice that they seek for no excuses to palliate his conduct, and have no condemnation for this ruthless destroyer of Iskander's happy home. But they are Muhammadans, and seldom allow themselves the luxury of burning moral convictions. I have never seen a missionary proselytising amongst the Malays, but many years ago I was told that a Christian missionary came to Malâya full of zeal and confident of success. He began with a man who seemed an earnest, truthful person, anxious to learn, a promising subject. The missionary told him the story of the Immaculate Conception. The Malay listened to the end, showing great interest in the miraculous narrative of the Blessed Virgin ; then he said, " If that had happened to my wife, I should have killed her."

XVII

# MALAY SUPERSTITIONS

> There are more things in heaven and
> earth, Horatio,
> Than are dreamt of in your philosophy
>
> *Hamlet*

MALAY superstitions are the survival of a time
antecedent to the advent of the gospel of
Islam, and their strong hold on the people is only
another proof of the conservative tendencies of the
race. What was the Faith of Malâya seven hundred
years ago it is hard to say, but there is a certain
amount of evidence to lead to the belief that it was
a form of Brahmanism and that no doubt had succeeded the original Spirit Worship.

I do not propose to attempt to enumerate all the
various forms of superstition, their name is legion,
but only to describe a few that are both curious and
interesting.

I have already referred to what is known as *bĕr-
hantu,* the practice of a kind of witchcraft for the

healing of the sick ; it reminds one of "casting out devils in the name of Beelzebub the Prince of the devils "—and I might here give some of the incantations commonly spoken by the exorcist, but one will suffice. Here is the translation of a most potent exorcism believed to be efficacious against the malevolent attacks of a thousand lesser demons :

Heigh! thou Spirit whose name is Jin Pari of the Jin Âruah ; Rabiah Jâmil was thy mother's, Imam Jâmil thy father's name ; thou art the grandchild of Hakim Baisuri, the great-grandchild of Mâlim of the Forest. Thou Spirit of the path Lôrin, Spirit of the rising ground Sri Permâtang, Spirit of the ant-hill known as "Piebald Horse." Heigh! you white ants Sekutânai, why do you, Sekutâpa, flying up stream make me think you are on your way down, and flying down stream give the impression that you are going to the interior ?

I know your origin, spawn of Hell's spouting flame ; do not any longer torment this person.

If you disobey, I will curse you by the name of the Most High, saying, " By the Grace of God, by the Grace of God, by the Grace of God."

The final threat to drive out the demon by using the name of the Almighty is curious as showing how the exorcist seeks by a judicious blending of tradition with his latter-day Faith to get the better of the tormentor.

A very widespread superstition is that certain persons have familiar spirits who will, at the instance of their owners, enter into and plague any one whom it may be desired to injure. These evil spirits are known as *Bâjang*, *Pôlong*, *Pĕlsit*, and *Langsûior*, the last being a female spirit. They are either inherited or acquired by the practice of witch-craft, and the way in which their possession is brought home to any member of the community is as little reasonable as the " proof" of the exercise of similar powers in the Western witch not so many centuries ago.

Some one in a village falls ill of a complaint, the symptoms of which are unusual ; there may be convulsions, unconsciousness, or delirium, possibly for some days together or with intervals between the attacks. The relatives will call in a native doctor, and at her (she is usually an ancient female) suggestion, or without it, an impression will arise that the patient is the victim of a *bâjang*. Such an impression quickly develops into certainty and any trifle will suggest the owner of the evil spirit. One method of verifying this suspicion is to wait till the patient is in a state of delirium and then to question him or her as to who is the author of the trouble. This should be done by some independent person of authority who is supposed to be able to ascertain the truth.

A further and convincing proof is then to call in a "*Pawang*" skilled in dealing with wizards (in Malay countries they are usually men), and if he knows his business his power is such that he will place the sorcerer in one room, and, while he in another scrapes an iron vessel with a razor, the culprit's hair will fall off as though the razor had been applied to his head instead of to the vessel ! That is supposing he *is* the culprit; if not, of course he will pass through the ordeal without damage.

I have been assured that the shaving process is so efficacious that, as the vessel represents the head of the person standing his trial, wherever it is scraped, the wizard's hair will fall off in a corresponding spot. It might be supposed that under these circumstances the accused is reasonably safe, but this test of guilt is not always employed. What more commonly happens is that when several cases of unexplained sickness have occurred in a village, with possibly one or two deaths, the people of the place lodge a formal complaint against the supposed author of these ills and desire that he be punished.

Before the advent of British influence it was the practice to kill the wizard or witch whose guilt had been established to Malay satisfaction, and such executions were carried out not very many years ago.

I remember a case in Perak less than ten years ago when the people of an up-river village accused a man of keeping a *bâjang*, and the present Sultan, who was then the principal Malay Judge in the State, told them he would severely punish the *bâjang* if they would produce it. They went away hardly satisfied and shortly after made a united representation to the effect that if the person suspected were allowed to remain in their midst they would kill him. Before anything could be done they put him, his family, and effects on a raft and started them down the river. On their arrival at Kuala Kangsar the man was given an isolated hut to live in, but not long afterwards he disappeared.

The hereditary *bâjang* comes like other evils, the unsought heritage of a dissolute ancestry, but the acquired *bâjang* is usually obtained from the newly-buried body of a stillborn child, which is supposed to be the abiding-place of a familiar spirit until lured therefrom by the solicitations of someone who, at dead of night, stands over the grave and by potent incantations persuades the *bâjang* to come forth.

*Pôlong* and *Pĕlsit* are but other names for *Bâjang*, the latter is chiefly used in the State of Kĕdah where it is considered rather *chic* to have a *pĕlsit*. A Kĕdah lady the other day, eulogising the advantages of possessing a familiar spirit (she said that amongst other things it gave her absolute control over her husband and the power of annoying people who offended her), thus described the method of securing this useful ally :

" You go out," she said, " on the night before the full moon and stand with your back to the moon and your face to an ant-hill so that your shadow falls on the ant-hill. Then you recite certain *jampi* (incantations), and bending forward try to embrace your shadow. If you fail try again several times, repeating more incantations. If not successful go the next night and make a further effort, and the night after if necessary—three nights in all. If you cannot then catch your shadow, wait till the same day on the following month and renew the attempt. Sooner or later you will succeed, and, as you stand there in the brilliance of the moonlight, you will see that you have drawn your shadow into yourself, and your body will never again cast a shade. Go home and in the night, whether sleeping or waking, the form of a child will appear before you and put out its tongue ; that seize and it will remain while the rest of the child disappears. In a little while the tongue will turn into something that breathes, a small animal, reptile or insect, and when you see the creature has life put it in a bottle and the *pĕlsit* is yours."

It sounds easy enough, and one is not surprised to hear that everyone in Kĕdah, who is anybody, keeps a *pĕlsit.*

*Langsûior*, the female familiar, differs hardly at all from the *bâjang* except that she is a little more baneful, and, when under the control of a man, he sometimes becomes the victim of her attractions, and she will even bear him elfin children.

It is all very well for the Kĕdah ladies to sacrifice their shadows to obtain possession of a *pĕlsit,* leaders of society must be in the fashion at any cost ; but there are plenty of people living in Perak who have seen more than one ancient Malay dame taken out into the river, and, despite her protestations, her tears and entreaties, have watched her, with hands

and feet tied, put into the water and slowly pushed
down out of sight by means of a long pole with a
fork at one end which fitted on to her neck. Those
who witnessed these executions have no doubt of
the justice of the punishment, and not uncommonly
add that after two or three examples had been made
there would always ensue a period of rest from the
torments of the *bâjang*. I have also been assured
that the *bâjang*, in the shape of a lizard, has been
seen to issue from the drowning person's nose.
That statement, no doubt, is made on the authority
of those who condemned and executed the victim.

The following legend gives the Malay conception
of the origin of all *Jin*, *hantu*, *bâjang*, and other
spirits.

The Creator determined to make Man, and for
that purpose He took some clay from the earth and
fashioned it into the figure of a man. Then He
took the Spirit of Life to endue this body with
vitality and placed the spirit on the head of the
figure. But the spirit was strong, and the body,
being only clay, could not hold it and was reft in
pieces and scattered into the air. Those fragments
of the first great Failure are the spirits of earth and
sea and air.

The Creator then formed another clay figure, but

into this one He wrought some iron, so that when it received the vital spark it withstood the strain and became Man. That man was Adam, and the iron that is in the constitution of his descendants has stood them in good stead. When they lose it, they become of little more account than their proto-type the first failure.

Another article of almost universal belief is that the people of a small State in Sumatra called Korinchi have the power of assuming at will the form of a tiger, and in that disguise they wreak vengeance on those they wish to injure. Not every Korinchi man can do this, but still the gift of this strange power of metamorphosis is pretty well confined to the people of the small Sumatran State. At night when respectable members of society should be in bed, the Korinchi man slips down from his hut, and, assuming the form of a tiger, goes about "seeking whom he may devour."

I have heard of four Korinchi men arriving in a district of Perak, and that night a number of fowls were taken by a tiger. The strangers left and went further up country, and shortly after only three of them returned and stated that a tiger had just been killed, and they begged the local headman to bury it !

On another occasion some Korinchi men appeared and sought hospitality in a Malay house, and there also the fowls disappeared in the night, and there were unmistakable traces of the visit of a tiger, but the next day one of the visitors fell sick, and shortly after vomited chicken-feathers!

It is only fair to say that the Korinchi people strenuously deny the tendencies and the power ascribed to them, but aver that they properly belong to the inhabitants of a district called Chenâku in the interior of the Korinchi country. Even there, however, it is only those who are practised in the *elĕmu sĕhir*, the occult arts who are thus capable of transforming themselves into tigers, and the Korinchi people profess themselves afraid to enter the Chenâku district.

It was my misfortune some years ago to be robbed of some valuable property, and several Malay friends strongly advised me to take the advice of an astrologer or other learned person who (so they said) would be able to give the name of the thief, and probably recover most of the stolen things. I fear that I had no great faith in this method of detection, but I was anxious to see what could be done, for the East is a curious place, and no one with an inquiring mind can have lived in it long without seeing phenomena that are not always explained by modern text-books on Natural Philosophy.

I was first introduced to an Arab of very remarkable appearance. He was about fifty years old, tall, with pleasant features and extraordinary grey-blue eyes, clear and far-seeing, a man of striking and impressive personality. I was travelling when I met him, and tried to persuade him to return with me, but that he said he could not do, though he promised to follow me by an early steamer. He said he would be able to tell me all about the robbery, who committed it, where the stolen property then was, and that all he would want was an empty house wherein he might fast in solitude for three days, without which preparation, he said, he would not be able to see what he sought. He told me that after his vigil, fast, and prayer, he would lay in his hand a small piece of paper on which there would be some writing, into this he would pour a little water, and in that extemporised mirror he would see a vision of the whole transaction. He declared that, after gazing intently into this divining-glass, the inquirer first recognised the figure of a little old man. That having duly saluted this *Jin*, it was only necessary to ask him to conjure up the scene of the robbery, when all the details would be re-enacted in the liquid glass under the eyes of the gazer, who would there and then describe all that he saw. I had heard all this before, only it had been stated to me then that the medium through whose eyes the vision could alone be seen must be a young child of such tender years that it could have never told a lie! The Arab, however, professed himself not only able to conjure up the scene, but to let me see it for myself, if I would follow his directions. Unfortunately, my grey-eyed friend failed to keep his promise, and I never met him again.

A local Chief, however, declared his power to read the past by this method, if only he could find the truthful child. In this he appeared to succeed, but when, on the following day, he came to disclose to me the results of his skill, he said that a difficulty had arisen because just when the child (a little boy) was beginning to relate what he saw he suddenly became unconscious, and it took the astrologer two hours to restore him to his normal state. All the mothers of tender-aged and possibly truthful children declined after this to lend their offspring for the ordeal.

My friend was not, however, at the end of his

resources, and, though only an amateur in divina-
tion, he undertook to try by other methods to find
the culprit. For this purpose he asked me to give
him the names of everyone in the house at the time
the robbery was committed. I did so, and the next
day he gave me one of those names as that of the
thief. I asked how he had arrived at this knowledge,
he described the method and consented to repeat
the experiment in my presence. That afternoon I
went with him to a small house belonging to his sister.
Here I found my friend the Chief, his sister, and
two men whom I did not recognise. We all sat in a
very small room, the Chief in the centre with a copy
of the Korân on a reading-stand, near to him the
two men, opposite to each other, the sister against
one wall and I in a corner. A clean new unglazed
earthenware bowl with a wide rim was produced.
This was filled with water, and a piece of fair white
cotton cloth tied over the top, making a surface like
that of a drum.

I was asked to write the name of each person
present in the house when the robbery was committed on a small piece of paper, and to fold each
paper up so that all should be alike, and then to
place one of the names on the cover of the vessel.
I did so, and the proceedings began by the two

men placing each the middle joint of the fore-finger of his right hand under the rim of the bowl on opposite sides, and so supporting it about six inches above the floor. The vessel being large and full of water was heavy, and the men supported the strain by resting their right elbows on their knees as they sat cross-legged on the floor and face to face. It was then that I selected one of the folded papers, and placed it on the cover of the vessel. The Chief read a page of the Korân, and as nothing happened he said that was not the name of the guilty person, and I changed the paper for another. This occurred four times, but at the fifth the reading had scarcely commenced when the bowl began to slowly turn round from left to right, the supporters letting their hands go round with it, until it twisted itself out of their fingers and fell on the floor with a considerable bang and a great spluttering of water through the thin cover. "That," said the Chief, "is the name of the thief."

It was the name of the person already mentioned by him.

I did not, however, impart that piece of information to the company, but went on to the end of my papers, nothing more happening.

I said I should like to try the test again, and as

the Chief at once consented we began afresh, and this time I put the name of the suspected person on first, and once more the vessel turned round and twisted itself out of the hands of the holders, till it fell on the floor and I was surprised it did not break. After trying a few more I said I was satisfied, and the ordeal of the bowl was over.

Then the Chief asked me whose name had been on the vessel when it moved, and I told him. It was a curious coincidence certainly. I wrote the names in English, which no one could read ; moreover, I was so placed that no one could see what I wrote, and they none of them attempted to do so. Then the papers were folded up so as to be all exactly alike, they were shuffled together, and I did not know one from the other till I looked inside myself. Each time I went from my corner and placed a name on the vessel already held on the fingers of its supporters. No one except I touched the papers, and no one but the Chief ever spoke till the *séance* was over. I asked the men who held the bowl why they made it turn round at that particular moment, but they declared they had nothing to do with it, and that the vessel twisted itself off their fingers against their inclination.

...The name disclosed by this experiment was

certainly that of the person whom there was most
reason to suspect, but beyond that I learnt nothing.

Another plan for surprising the secret of a
suspected person is to get into the room where that
person is sleeping, and after making certain passes
to question the slumberer, when he may truthfully
answer all the questions put to him. This is a
favourite device of the suspicious husband.

Yet another plan is to place in the hand of a
*pâwang*, magician, or medium, a divining-rod formed
of three lengths of rattan tied together at one end,
and when he gets close to the person " wanted," or
to the place where anything stolen is concealed, the
rod vibrates in a remarkable manner.

A great many Malays and one or two Europeans
may be found who profess to have seen water
drawn from a *kris*. The *modus operandi* is simple.
The " pàwang " (I dare not call him conjurer)
works with bare arms to show there is no deception.
He takes the *kris* (yours, if you prefer it) from its
wooden handle, and, holding the steel point downwards in his left hand, he recites a short incantation
to the effect that he knows all about iron and where
it comes from, and that it must obey his orders. He
then with the thumb and first two fingers of his
right hand proceeds to gently squeeze the steel,

moving his fingers up and down the blade. After a little while a few drops of water fall from the point of the *kris*, and these drops quickly develop into a stream that will fill a cup. The " pâwang " will then hand round the blade and tell you to bend it ; this you will find no difficulty in doing, but by making two or three passes over the *kris* the " pâwang " can render it again so hard that it cannot be bent.

The only drawback to this trick or miracle is that the process ruins the temper of the steel, and a *kris* that has been thus treated is useless.

One evening I was discussing these various superstitions with the Sultan of Perak, and I did not notice that the spiritual teacher of His Highness had entered and was waiting to lead the evening prayer. The *guru*, or teacher, no doubt heard the end of our conversation and was duly scandalised, for the next day I received from him a letter, of which the following is the translation :

" First praise to God, the Giver of all good, a Fountain of Compassion to His servants.

" From Haji Wan Muhammad, Teacher of His Highness the Sultan of Perak, to the Resident who administers the Government of Perak.

" The whole earth is in the hand of the most
High God, and He gives it as an inheritance to
whom He will of His subjects. The true religion
is also of God, and Heaven is the reward of those
who fear the Most High. Salvation and peace are
for those who follow the straight path, and only
they will in the end arrive at real greatness. No
Raja can do good, and none can be powerful except
by the help of God the Most High, who is also
Most Mighty.

" I make ten thousand salutations. I wish to
inquire about the practice of *bĕr-hantu*, driving
oneself mad and losing one's reason, as has been
the custom of Rajas and Chiefs in this State of
Perak ; is it right according to your religion, Mr.
Resident, or is it not ? For that practice is a
deadly sin to the Muhammadan Faith, because
those who engage in it lose their reason and waste
their substance for nothing ; some of them cast it
into the water, while others scatter it broadcast
through the jungle. How is such conduct treated
by your religion, Mr. Resident, is it right or wrong ?
I want you in your indulgence to give me an answer,
for this practice is very hard on the poor. The
Headmen collect from the *rayats*, and then they
make elaborate preparations of food, killing a buffalo

or fowls, and all this is thrown away as already stated. According to the Muhammadan religion such proceedings lead to destruction.

"I salute you many times, do not be angry, for I do not understand your customs, Mr. Resident.

"(Signed) HAJI MUHAMMAD ABU HASSAN."

# XVIII

# WITH A CASTING-NET

Where fountains of sweet water run
between,
And sun and shadow chequer-chased
the green

JÁMI

PERAK is one of the largest and most populous of the States of the Malay Peninsula, it is the one where probably the rulers can claim the clearest genealogy and the longest recorded descent, and it is unquestionably here that all ancient rites and customs have been most carefully preserved.

Whilst it was to Perak that the first British Resident was appointed, and this State is now the most wealthy, advanced, and prosperous of all those under British influence, the Malays still maintain their traditions and observe their honoured customs as though railways and steamers, education and sanitation had no more part in their lives than when Albuquerque was striving to effect a landing on the shores of Malacca.

For ages it has been a practice of the Sultans of Perak to reserve certain waters for their own fishing, and certain jungle tracts (usually surrounding a hot spring of mineral water) for their own hunting. There they would resort, annually or oftener, and with their relatives, chiefs, and followers take their kingly pleasure, as it was duly chronicled had been the custom of their ancestors.

In the lull after the first heavy rains, that is about the month of December, when the river has been swollen to flood-height for a couple of months, the *tuntong* or river-turtles ascend the Perak River in considerable numbers and lay their eggs on certain convenient sand stretches in the neighbourhood of Bota, about 100 miles from the river's mouth.

The most frequented of these laying grounds is a place called *Pâsir Tĕlor* (egg-sand), just below Bota, and it is here that the ladies of the Court annually assemble to dig up the eggs, which the Malay considers one of the greatest delicacies known to him.

The river-turtle is a great deal smaller than the sea-turtle, but it lays a larger egg, and one much more valued by Malays.

As soon as the river rises watchers are stationed on the sands, and the turtles are said to lay three times. The nests are dug between two and three feet under the sand, and contain from about fifteen to thirty-five eggs each. During the laying season boats are not allowed to stop at the sands for fear they should disturb the turtles.

When the first set of eggs has been laid and the turtles have returned to the river, the watchers open the nests and send the eggs up to the Sultan. The second set of nests is opened by the royal party, and the third is left to hatch, an operation that takes six months. There is no sitting, the young turtles simply emerge from the sand, walk down into the river and swim away.

It is said that if the first and second nests are left untouched, the turtles themselves open them and scatter and destroy the eggs ; but that, after the third "lay," they take their departure, having accomplished their task.

Directly the watchers report that the turtles have made the second nests, the Sultan and his family, with the neighbouring chiefs and their families, take boat and paddle down the stream to Pâsir Telor.

Fifteen or twenty large house-boats and several

bamboo rafts containing about one hundred and fifty people make an imposing procession. The rafts are simply floating houses, with mat walls and a high thatched roof, and are manned by crews of from four to sixteen polers; but the boats are graceful and picturesque barges, of which the foundation is a long dug-out of hard wood drawing very little water, the freeboard is raised by the breadth of one or two planks, and over the stern half of the boat is built a palm-thatched covering on a slight wooden frame, while curtains secure privacy. Inside this house, the roof of which rises in a sharp curve towards the stern, sit and lie on mats and cushions the owner and his family or friends. The crew occupy the forward half of the boat, where they sit to paddle down stream or stand to pole up. The steersman has a high seat in the stern, from whence he is able to see clear of the cabin-roof.

The covered portion of the barge which carries the Sultan's principal wife is decorated with six scarlet-bordered white umbrellas. Two officers stand all day long, just outside the state-room, holding open black umbrellas with silver fringes, and two others are in the bows with long bamboo poles held close together and erect. The royal bugler sits on the extreme end of the prow, and from time to time blows a call on the antique silver trumpet of the regalia. Flags are flown, other boats carry gongs and drums, and altogether the pleasure-fleet makes a brave show and a considerable noise, attracting the attention of all the dwellers on the riverine.

The journey from the Sultan's palace at Kuala Kangsar occupies two days, and on the morning of the third all the ladies of the party, with all their attendants and children (a good many still in arms), disembark for the ceremony of digging out the turtle-eggs.

The ladies are in their smartest garments and wear their costliest jewels. It is a blaze of brilliant-coloured silks, of painted *sârongs*, cloth-of-gold scarves, and embroidered gauze veils ; of bright sunshades, gold bracelets, necklaces, and bangles ; of curious jewelled brooches, massive hair-pins, and rings flashing with the light of diamonds and rubies.

The men appear in jackets, trousers, and *sârongs* of hardly less striking hues ; but the horror of Western dyes and Western schemes of colour has not yet demoralised the Malay's innate sense of beauty and fitness, and nothing offends the eye as all this wealth of bravery moves slowly across the strand.

A scorching sun shines down on the gaily-clad figures with their background of dark jungle, on the yellow sands and sparkling river, with its burden of picturesque boats, and gives light and shadow to a charming picture.

The watchers have marked with twigs the various nests, and each lady of rank, with her little crowd of attendants, makes for one of these, and with her hands begins to dig up the sand in search of the eggs. But the nest is deep down, and the sides of the hole have a way of falling in on the digger, so a man or boy is desired to remove the overburden and make things easy for the lady. The overlying sand is quickly scooped out until one or two of the white eggs are disclosed, and then the lady, sitting on the edge and stooping far down, can just manage to reach the nest, and the eggs are carefully handed up.

Besides the pleasure of actually removing the eggs with one's own hand, of displaying to admiring eyes a vision of taper fingers and rounded wrist, of showing how little it matters that the costliest garments should trail in the sand, there is the rivalry of whose nest yields the largest number of eggs. Anything over twenty-five is considered a satisfactory find.

By the time all the nests have been rifled, the sands are growing so hot under the rays of the fiery sun that bare feet can hardly endure what is little short of torture. There is an almost hurried return to the boats, the finery is exchanged for simpler garments, and all the men and many of the ladies take to the river, and there disport themselves in a manner that is refreshing to sun-scorched bodies and the eyes of the Western spectator who is fortunate enough to see how it is possible to be unconventionally natural and yet perfectly modest.

It is only on such occasions as this that a strange man can see these ladies unveiled and even so he is not expected to look at them or go very near them ; but their bathing-costume differs hardly at all from that which they commonly wear, and they thoroughly enjoy this opportunity of revelling in the clear waters of the sand-bedded stream.

Then every one scrambles back into the boats, which are pushed off into deep water, the rowers seize their paddles and with beat of gong and the musical notes of the silver *serûnai*, with jest and laughter, pennons waving, and bright eyes sparkling behind the rainbow-coloured blinds, the picturesque flotilla glides on its course down the long sunny reach, in and out amongst the islets, round a heavily-wooded, deeply-shadowed headland, past the riverside hamlets and the orchards, the stately palms, the clusters of bamboo that overhang the water like great plumes of pale green feathers, and so ever onward through sunlight and shadow till another bourne is reached.

The graceful turn of the leading barge towards a sand-spit flanked by a long inviting backwater, the roll of a drum and every prow is headed for the shallows of the bank that divides the *âyer mâti,* the " dead water," from the living hurrying stream.

The boats arrange themselves in divisions, the crews land, make fires, and boil the rice for their mid-day meal, while the cooking and breakfasting of the members of the " court" is done on board the various barges.

In this feudal and conservative country when the people eat they *mâkan,* but the Raja does not *mâkan,* with him it is *santap.* When "the masses" bathe they *mandi,* but the same operation in the case of a Raja is called *sêram ;* a chief or a beggar may sleep and that is *tîdor,* but when the Raja sleeps he is said to *bêr-âdu.* This does not mean that a wide gulf divides Malay classes, there is rather that communion as of the members of an old Scotch clan, but respect and courtesy are characteristic of the race, a prized legacy which it is not yet considered a sign of either independence or good manners to despise. People of the same class, rajas and chiefs, children and parents, brothers and sisters, speak to each other with studied deference and never forget the little distinctions that mark fine shades of rank or age. Boys and girls are as careful in the observance of these courtesies as are their elders.

Education and contact with Europeans will alter all this, and in the next century there will be more equality and probably less politeness and fraternity. But then also there will be no royal preserves, no class privileges, and no State junketings where noble and peasant meet in generous rivalry of skill with a single desire to snatch from the toil, the disappointments, and the sorrows of life one week of pleasure wherein individual joy may grow greater in the knowledge that it is shared by many.

Future possibilities do not disturb our friends, whose guiding principle is rather " insufficient for the day is the pleasure thereof." They have attacks of hatred and gloom, and then they kill, if the desire is strong enough, but these fits are rare, and when not actively engaged in amusing themselves they are lotus-eating, sometimes figuratively, sometimes in reality.

This is a time for action, and, the mid-day meal disposed of, all the men of the party get ready their casting-nets and don the garments that will least hamper the free use of their limbs and will not be injured by a thorough wetting.

The backwater has a narrow and shallow entrance on the river, and this entrance is staked across to guard it from what in the West would be called poachers. Through the stakes a way has now been made wide enough to admit of the passage of boats. The Sultan's barge and a few other house-boats have passed the barrier, and these are accompanied by a fleet of fifty uncovered dug-outs, each with a light grating of split-bamboos over half its length, and each carrying two or three paddlers, one of whom steers and one man standing on the extreme end of the bow ready to cast the net.

These nets are of local make, the mesh is small, the thread of twisted strands of finest cotton, and the length varies according to the ability of the owner to cast it. A very short net is five or six cubits in length from centre to edge, a long one is twelve or thirteen cubits, and to cast that with accuracy so that it reaches the water perfectly extended requires a very skilful hand. The bottom or edge of the net is weighted with small leaden rings that sink it rapidly through the water, while a fine cord from the centre is attached to the right wrist of the thrower. The net is usually dyed a dark brown with a solution made from the bark of the mangrove.

The backwater where this annual netting is done is a long narrow strip of fairly deep water widening slightly in the centre and contracting at the ends. On one side it is bordered by a low grass-grown shore and on the other by a jungle-covered bank from which the overhanging branches cast dark shadows on the glassy surface, stirred here and there into tiny wavelets by every passing zephyr.

By 3 P.M. all is ready; some of the oldest and most skilful netters stand in the bows of the royal barges, a dozen young rajas are in dug-outs and the others are occupied by their owners, men from the neighbouring villages who have come to join in the sport.

The Sultan gives the signal, and the boats move off slowly and at once form themselves into a crescent, with the royal barges in the centre. The horns of the crescent draw towards each other, the boats make a simultaneous in-turn, the circle is completed, and at the moment when it becomes sufficiently circumscribed every net is cast, covering the whole surface of the water within the ring of boats. Directly the nets have been cast they sink, the paddlers back-water, and each net is slowly drawn to the surface and the fish taken are disengaged from the fine meshes and thrown into the boat under the bamboo grating.

Almost every net contains fish, and the numbers vary from two or three to fifty or sixty bright silvery fishes weighing from half a pound to a pound each.

The operation is then repeated, and the fleet of boats works its way slowly from end to end of the backwater, a distance of about a mile.

Sometimes every net makes a good haul, sometimes only one or two do very well, and all the rest indifferently. It is no easy matter with such an insecure foothold to cast a long and heavy net, but, well done, the act of casting is graceful and attractive. First the slack of the cord is taken up in loops in the right hand and after it the net, until the leaden rings clear the boat and reach to about the thrower's knee. Then with his left hand he takes up part of the skirt of the net and hangs it over his right arm and shoulder. This done he seizes the balance of the skirt in his left hand, swings his body backwards and then forwards with a strong propelling movement of arm, shoulder, and back that sends the net straight out over the water to fall perfectly extended, like a huge brown cobweb, the outer edges sinking instantly under the weight of the leaden rings and drawing together by reason of the resistance of the inner surface of the net.

The game *looks* easy enough, but try it and you will probably find yourself in the water at the first cast with the net tied up into an inextricable knot.

Watch the experienced hand. The boats are now at a bend in the middle of the backwater, the circle is formed, the in-turn is given to the bows, the ring narrows, and at this moment the scene is picturesque to a degree and strangely weird.

Atmospheric changes come quickly here ; the sky has become suddenly overcast, a heavy rain-cloud is being rapidly driven before a rising wind, and the water is now dark and gloomy. This *cordon* of low black boats, so close to each other that they almost touch, on every bow a half-bent, quaintly-clad form with the net hanging in graceful folds from arm and shoulder, while fifty dark earnest faces gaze eagerly on the narrowing space. In that instant it flashes across the spectator's mind that some mystic rite of fell intent is to be performed within that magic zone. Then heigh! Abracadabra! The word is given to cast, and from fifty boats the nets fly out with a swirl and settle on the water with a gentle hiss. But the skilful thrower waits for a second or two, knowing that the fish, frightened by this rain of lead, will dash for the only spot where there seems to be a gap. Then deftly he casts a net with a diameter of forty feet, and the moment he strains the cord he realises that he has made an extraordinary capture. He pulls the net up a little way, and then, plunging his arms into the water, grasps the meshes on either side and calls for help to raise the struggling mass of fish. All eyes are fixed on the lucky Raja, and as the take is lifted into the boat there are shouts of delight and congratulation and clapping of hands from the ladies, who are keenly interested. By this single cast the thrower has secured one hundred and twenty-one fish, and his contribution for the afternoon is over seven hundred " tails."

Just as the furthest end of the backwater is reached the rain, which has been long threatening, comes down in torrents, and there is a race for shelter and dry clothes. The dug-outs with three or four paddlers easily beat the barges with a dozen, but long before the river is reached the netters are as wet as the fish, and have a swim in the warm water of the river before changing into dry clothes.

Then there is a lull in the storm, and the more enthusiastic return to the netting and, unmindful of hunger, darkness, and rain, still cast the nets till 10 P.M., when they return thoroughly tired out, but happy in the knowledge that the bag numbers over ten thousand fish.

Amongst these late comers and most ardent sportsmen are several ladies who, not satisfied with the ease and dignity of a royal barge, have braved the elements and gone fasting to share the excitement of the netting in the discomfort of the dugouts.

That is how the Sultan of Perak's annual fishing party takes its pleasure, and about the very same time His Highness of Păhang will be leading a similar expedition in the quiet waters of an old channel of the Păhang River.

There, however, the method is rather different— the water is poisoned with the juice of the *tuba* root, and the stupefied fish are speared and netted as they float and swim aimlessly about. The fun is much the same, perhaps, but the pursuit is less sporting than by the means employed in Perak. It is not however, perfectly easy to spear even drugged fish without both skill and practice.

In Păhang, also, the pageant is conducted with much state and ancientry, and, as the nature of the pastime requires only a moderate effort, the ladies of the Harîm smile on the proceedings and, armed with silken nets on hafts of gold, themselves essay to scoop up the scaly quarry. Amongst the ladies of the Court are some the exceeding fairness of whose skin, the perfect oval of their faces, and the glances of their liquid eyes so embarrass the men of the party that many a spear flies wide of its mark.

There are some things still hidden from the ken of Cook and the race of Globe trotters, and I do not fear to reveal the secrets of this remote corner of the earth, for, if any be thereby induced to visit the Peninsula in search of such displays as I have tried to describe, he will meet with disappointment.

You cannot, in the language of Western culture, put a penny in the slot and set in motion the wheels of this barbarous Eastern figure.

# XIX

# JAMES WHEELER WOODFORD BIRCH

Such was our friend, formed on the
good old plan,
A true and brave and downright
honest man

WHITTIER

ON the 2nd November 1875, Mr. James
Wheeler Woodford Birch, British Resident
of Perak, was assassinated by Malays at a place
called Pâsir Sâlak on the Perak River. I propose
to describe why and how this murder was committed.

Mr. Birch began life as a midshipman in the
Royal Navy. He abandoned the sea for Government employment in Ceylon, where he spent the
best years of his life, and was promoted to be Government Agent of the Eastern Province, one of the
highest positions in the Island. In 1870 Mr. Birch
was appointed Colonial Secretary of the Straits
Settlements, and when Major-General Sir Andrew

Clarke, R.E., then Governor of the Straits Settlements, concluded the Pangkor Treaty with the Perak Chiefs in 1874 and introduced a new departure in the relations between the British Government and the Malay States, he selected Mr. Birch for the difficult post of adviser to the Sultan of Perak.

Mr. Birch assumed his duties in the end of 1874, and very soon found that, looking to the people with whom he had to deal and his own powerlessness to enforce an order, he had undertaken a well-nigh impossible task. At that time the Malay Peninsula was a *terra incognita* to white men, and the characteristics, customs, peculiarities and prejudices of the Malay had yet to be learnt.

Of all the States in the Peninsula Perak was probably the least well suited for the schooling of a Resident and the initiation of the interesting but dangerous experiment of Government by the advice of a British officer.

It had a large Malay population, people whose ancestors had for generations belonged to the place and who were saturated with ancient customs, prejudices, and superstitions that had to be learned, and with many of which it was difficult to sympathise. It had an unusual number of Rajas and Chiefs, each with some kind of privilege or vested interest. The revolting practice of debt-slavery, under which the slaves often suffered indescribable wrongs, was rife in the land, and, though contrary to the Muhammadan religion, was supported and clung to by all the upper classes. The State was torn by internal dissensions, the jealousies and rivalries of opposing claimants to the Sultanship and other high offices. The rivers and jungle tracks were the only means of getting about the country. The white man was an unknown and unfeared quantity.

Mr. Birch, unfortunately, for all his long Eastern experience, knew very little of Malays and almost nothing of their language, and, though he always had with him a very capable Malay interpreter, the inability to carry on a direct conversation with chiefs and people greatly increased his difficulties. He was not, however, the man to sit down in the face of opposition either to save himself trouble or to acknowledge defeat, and the consequence was that his extraordinary energy in travelling about the country, " spying out the land," and his persistence in attempting to redress grievances, to save lives, to bring the guilty to punishment, and to induce the then Sultan Abdullah and his immediate following to mend their ways, earned him the determined opposition of all those who disliked interference, and preferred the state of uncontrolled lawlessness to which they were accustomed.

Mr. Birch lived in Perak as its Resident for barely twelve months, but to trace with care the reasons why his relations with Abdullah grew daily more strained till matters culminated in the assassination of the Resident, would be to write a volume. It is sufficient to state a few of the more prominent facts.

First, it is necessary to say in the most positive terms that Mr. Birch was assassinated solely and entirely for political reasons, for the reasons I have already given. He was white, he was a Christian and a stranger, he was restless, climbed hills and journeyed all over the country, he interfered with murderers and other evil-doers, he constantly bothered the Sultan about business and kept pressing him to introduce reforms, while every change is regarded by the Malay with suspicion and distrust. That was his crime in their eyes; of personal feeling there was none, wherever Mr. Birch went there were people who had to thank him for some kindness, some attention. The Malays have always admitted this, and, if it seems strange that I should make a point of the motive, it is because Europeans who did not know have suggested that the Resident's murder was due to non-political causes, a suggestion for which there is not a semblance of foundation.

By September 1875, matters had come to a dead-lock. With the Resident, in what was called the down-stream country, was a Sultan, Abdullah, created by the British Government, but declining to accept the advice of the Resident who had been appointed at his special request. Abdullah's opposition was mainly negative but absolutely effective, for as the Resident could only tender advice and had no commission, and no sufficient means to compel its adoption, his voice was that of one " crying in the wilderness." Up-stream there was another Sultan, Ismail, elected by some of the chiefs but admitted to have no sufficient claim to the post. Between the partisans of these rival Sultans, very strained relations existed.

Then there was another claimant to the Sultan-ship in the person of the Raja Muda Jusuf, who lived still further up country, and while his claims were undoubtedly the best, his personal unpopu-larity was so great that the people would not accept him as Sultan.

The success of the Residential idea (for no one had attempted to formulate any scheme or system) depended on the existence of mutual confidence and friendship between Sultan and Resident. That was, unfortunately, wanting, and, as after many months of patient effort on the part of Mr. Birch the desired result seemed further away than ever, the governor of the neighbouring colony (then Major-General Sir W. Jervois, R.E.) determined to visit Perak and see what chance there was of establishing administrative authority, collecting revenue, and otherwise carrying out the provisions of the Pangkor Treaty.

As the result of that visit and of interviews between the Governor and the Chiefs, a proposition was made to Sultan Abdullah that the government of the State should be carried on in his name by British officers. He hesitated for some days, but, finding that the Raja Muda and others had at once and gladly accepted the suggestion, he determined to do the same, fearing, no doubt, that otherwise he might be left out of the administration altogether.

It was the Malay fasting-month, the *bûlan puâsa*, when these last events occurred. It is not an auspicious time for conducting negotiations with Malays, they do not even attempt to work for that month, they sleep for most of the day and sit up most of the night, eating and talking, discussing affairs and hatching plots. This, at least, is the case with the upper classes, and it is they only who are concerned in political movements ; the common people do not fast as a rule, and leave the plotting to the chiefs, whose business they think it is to scheme and to direct, theirs to obey.

In Lower Perak during this particular month of Ramthân, an unusual amount of discussion had been carried on between Sultan Abdullah and his chiefs, and they determined not only that the British Resident should be got rid of, but one of them, entitled the Maharaja Lela, undertook to do the business the next time Mr. Birch visited him.

This man, the Maharaja Lela, was a chief of considerable rank, after the Sultan he was the seventh in the State.   He lived at Pâsir Sâlak, on the right bank of the Perak River, about thirty miles above the residence of Sultan Abdullah, and about forty below that of ex-Sultan Ismail.   He avoided Mr. Birch whenever it was possible (though living only five miles from him), and managed to keep friends with both Sultans.

During the month, Sultan Abdullah, who was then with his boats at Pâsir Panjang, a couple of miles below the Maharaja Lela's house, summoned his chiefs and informed them that he had given over the government of the country to Mr. Birch. This announcement was received in silence by the others, to whom it was doubtless no news, but the Maharaja Lela said, "Even if your Highness has done so, I do not care at all. I will never acknowledge the authority of Mr. Birch or the white men. I have received letters from Sultan Ismail, the Měntri and the Pěnglima Kinta telling me on no account to obey the English Government in Perak. I will not allow Mr. Birch to set his foot in my kampong at Pâsir Sâlak."

The Sultan said, "Do you really mean that, Maharaja Lela?" and the Chief replied, "Truly I will not depart in the smallest degree from the old arrangement."

Another chief, the Datoh Sagor, who lived on the other side of the river, exactly opposite to Pâsir Sâlak, said, "What the Maharaja Lela does I will do."

The Sultan then got up and withdrew.

Two or three days before the end of the month the Sultan called another meeting of his chiefs at a place called Durian Sa'bâtang, ten miles below the small island on which the Resident's hut stood. At that meeting the Sultan produced the proclamations which were to be issued, placing the administration in the hands of British officers, and asked his chiefs what they thought of them. The Laksâmana, an influential chief, said, " Down here, in the lower part of the river, we must accept the proclamations " ; but the Maharaja Lela said, " In my kampong I will not allow any white man to post those proclamations. If they insist on doing so, there will certainly be a fight." To this the Sultan and other chiefs said, " Very well."

The Maharaja Lela immediately left, and having loaded his boats with rice, returned up river to his own kampong.

Pâsir Sâlak was the usual collection of Malay houses scattered about in groves of palm and fruit trees by the river-bank. Prominent amongst these was the Maharaja Lela's own dwelling, a large and comparatively new building of a more than ordin-arily substantial kind, round which he had for months past been digging a great ditch and throw-ing up a formidable earthwork crowned by a palisade. These preparations had been duly noted by the Resident.

Arrived at his own home, the Maharaja Lela sent out messengers to summon all the men in his immediate neighbourhood, and when they were collected he addressed them and stated that Mr.

Birch was coming up the river in a few days, and that, if he attempted to post any notices there, the orders of the Sultan and the down-river chiefs were to kill him. The assembled people said that, if those were the commands of the Sultan and the Maharaja Lela, they would carry them out. The chief then handed his sword to a man called Pandak Indut, his father-in-law, and directed that everyone should give to him the same obedience as to himself. The people then dispersed. It was one or two days after this that Mr. Birch arrived at Pâsir Sâlak.

Before describing the events of the 2nd November I must go back for a moment.

A number of officers, of whom I was one, had accompanied Sir W. Jervois in his journey to Perak. When the Governor and those with him left the State I was directed to remain behind with Mr. Birch to assist him in his negotiations with the chiefs. A fortnight later I went to Singapore with important papers and the drafts of proclamations defining the authority of the Resident under the new arrangement. These proclamations were printed, and I returned to Perak with them, joining Mr. Birch in his house on the 26th October.

I found the Resident had met with an accident ;

he had slipped down and so badly sprained his ankle that he could not walk without crutches. Lieut. Abbott, R.N., and four bluejackets were at Bandar Bharu (the Residency), where were also quartered the Sikh guard (about eighty men), the boatmen, and others.

Mr. Birch undertook to distribute the proclamations himself in the down-river districts, and directed me to go up river, to interview the ex-Sultan Ismail, the Raja Muda, the Raja Bendahara, and other up-country chiefs, and, having distributed the proclamations at all important villages from Kota Lama downwards, to try to meet him at Pâsir Sâlak on the 3rd November. There, he told me, he expected trouble for which he was quite prepared.

The Sikh guard was in a state bordering on mutiny in the evening of the 27th, but by the following morning they seemed to have returned to their senses, and about noon I left Bandar Bharu with two boats for the interior, Mr. Birch starting down stream at the same time.

He must have got through his part of the work more rapidly than he expected, for he reached Pâsir Sâlak with three boats at midnight on the 1st November, and anchored in midstream. The

1st November was the *Hâri Raya*, the first day after the Fast. At daylight his boats went alongside the bank, and the Resident's own boat was made fast to the floating bath-house of a Chinese jeweller, whose little shop stood on the high bank a few feet from the riverside. This was the only Chinese house in Pâsir Sâlak.

Mr. Birch was accompanied by Lieut. Abbott, an armed guard of twelve Sikhs, a Sikh orderly, the Malay interpreter (an eminently respectable Malay of nearly fifty named Muhammad Arshad), and a number of Malay boatmen and servants. There must have been about forty people in the party. Mr. Birch had with him a 3-Pr. brass gun, a small mortar, and a number of English fire-arms and Malay weapons, besides other property.

Directly after their arrival Mr. Abbott borrowed a small boat from the Chinaman and went across the river to Kampong Gajah to shoot snipe, the Chief of that place, the Dâtoh Sâgor, returning in the boat to Pâsir Sâlak, where he at once sought an interview with Mr. Birch.

After this conversation, which was held in the Resident's boat, the Dâtoh Sâgor and Mr. Birch's interpreter went to the Maharaja Lela's house, and the interpreter said to the Maharaja Lela that the

Resident wished to see him and would go to his house for that purpose, but if the Chief preferred it, and would go to Mr. Birch's boat, he would be glad to meet him there. The Maharaja Lela said, " I have nothing to do with Mr. Birch," and the interpreter returned to the boat and reported to his master the result of his interview.

The news of the Resident's arrival had been spread in every direction, and all those in the neighbourhood were ordered to come in. By this time, sixty or seventy men had assembled and were now standing about on the bank of the river close to Mr. Birch's boats. They were all armed with spears and *krises*, and Mr. Birch asked the Dâtoh Sâgor what they wanted, and that they should be told to stand further away. The Dâtoh told them to move away, and they gave a few yards, but at the same time began to abuse the Resident, calling him an "infidel," and asking what he meant by coming there asking questions and speaking like one in authority. Probably the Resident did not understand these ominous signs, but his boatmen heard and realised that trouble was brewing.

Mr. Birch now gave some proclamations to the interpreter, who took them on shore and posted them on the shutters of the Chinaman's shop.

Almost immediately, Pandak Indut, the Maharaja Lela's father-in-law, tore them down and took them off to the Maharaja Lela's house. That chief's dictum, was " Pull down the proclamations, and, if they persist in putting them up, kill them." Then it may be supposed he washed his hands of all responsibility, and Pandak Indut went out to execute his master's orders.

Meanwhile, Mr. Birch had handed to his interpreter some more proclamations to replace those removed, and, after giving directions to prepare his breakfast, went into the Chinaman's bath-house to bathe, leaving his Sikh orderly at the door with a loaded revolver. This bath-house was of the type common in Perak, two large logs floating in the stream, fastened together by cross-pieces of wood, and on them built a small house with mat sides about five feet high, and a roof closing on the sides but leaving two open triangular spaces at front and back. The structure is so moored that it floats parallel to the bank, and a person even standing up inside it cannot see what is taking place on the shore close by.

It was now about 10 A.M., and in spite of the threatening attitude of the large crowd of armed Malays standing in groups and passing between the river-bank and their chief's house, the Resident was composedly bathing in the river, while his people were some of them cooking on the bank, others sleeping in the boats, and a few, the Malays, anxiously expectant, fearing the signs boded a catastrophe.

They had not long to wait. The interpreter was still replacing the proclamations on the China-man's hut, when Pandak Indut and a number of other men came quickly from the Maharaja Lela's house.

The crowd asked, "What are the Chief's orders ?"

Pandak Indut replied, " He leaves the matter to me."

Going straight up to the Chinese shop, he began tearing down the newly-posted papers ; the inter-preter protested, and, seeing no heed was paid to him, turned towards the bath-house. He had not made half a dozen steps, when Pandak Indut over-took him and thrust his spear into the man's abdomen. The wounded man fell down the bank into the river and caught hold of his master's boat, but others followed him and cut him over the head and hands, so that he let go and struggled out into the stream.

The interpreter disposed of, Pandak Indut cried out, " Here is Mr. Birch in the bath-house, come, let us kill him," and, followed by three or four others shouting *âmok, âmok*, they leapt on to the floating timbers and thrust their spears through the open space in the front of the house.

At that time men in the boats could see Mr. Birch's head above the mat wall; it disappeared without any sound from him, and a moment after he came to the surface of the water astern of the house. Some of the murderers were already waiting there, and one of them, a man called Sipûtum, slashed the Resident over the head with a sword. He sank and was not seen again.

The Sikh orderly, standing with a revolver at the door of the bath-house, jumped into the river without any warning to his master, swam off to one of the boats and saved himself.

The river-bank was now the scene of a general *mêlee*. A Malay boatman and a Sikh had been killed, but the others had got one of the boats away from the bank into midstream and towards it two of Mr. Birch's Malays were swimming while they supported the grievously wounded interpreter. With difficulty they gained the boat and got the man in. As they dropped down the river Mr. Birch's coxswain urged the Sikhs to fire on the Malays, but they said they could not do so without an order ! He accordingly gave the order, and some shots were fired which for a moment cleared the bank. A small boat with two men in it put out lower down stream to intercept the fugitives, and two of them were wounded by shots from these men. The coxswain then wrenched a rifle from a Sikh and shot one of these assailants. After this the boat proceeded unmolested to Bandar Bharu. Long before they arrived there the interpreter died.

Mr. Abbott, shooting on the other bank, was warned of what had taken place, and with great difficulty got into a dug-out and made his way down stream under the fire of the Malays on the bank.

The attack, the murder of the Resident, his interpreter, the Sikh and the boatman, and the escape of the rest of the party was the work of a few minutes. Whilst still the passion of strife and bloodthirst swayed the crowd, the Maharaja Lela walked into their midst and asked whose hands had done the Resident and his men to death. Instantly Pandak Indut, Sipûtum, and the others, claimed credit for their murderous work. The Chief said, "It is well, none but those who struck blows can share in the spoil." He then called a man forward and said, " Go and tell the Laksamana that I have killed Mr. Birch." The message was delivered the same day, and the Laksamana said, " Very well, I will tell the Sultan."

That evening the Maharaja Lela sent a letter to ex-Sultan Ismail describing what he had done, and, to remove any doubt on the subject, he sent with it the Resident's own boat.

These are the facts about Mr. Birch's assassination, and it may be of some interest to add that the Resident's two boats were immediately rifled and all their contents carried up to the Maharaja Lela's house.

An attack upon the Residency was planned, ordered to be carried out that night, and a number of men started on the expedition, and even got within a few hundred yards of Bandar Bharu ; but it began to rain, and a man at whose house the party called told them they would get a warm reception, and it would be quite a different thing to murdering the Resident, so they elected to return with their object unattained.

By the help of a friendly Malay, a foreigner, Mr. Birch's body was recovered, brought to Bandar Bharu, and there buried on the night of the 6th November.

The Maharaja Lela and his neighbour the Dàtoh Sagor, having "burnt their ships," proceeded to stockade their villages, and those stockades were subsequently taken, the rebels driven out, and their villages destroyed.

Sooner or later punishment overtook every man directly concerned in this crime, and also nearly all those who were indirectly responsible. Some fell during the subsequent fighting, one died an outlaw in the jungle.

The first man captured was Sipûtum. He was brought in to Bandar Bharu late one evening in the early part of 1876, and I went to see him in the lock-up about midnight. A wilder looking creature it would have been hard to find. He was a *Pâwang*, a medicine man, a sorcerer. For many weeks he had been a hunted outcast, and he seemed to think that capture was almost preferable to the life he had been leading. He sat on the floor and described to me his share in Mr. Birch's murder, pausing between the sentences to kill mosquitoes on the wall of his cell. He volunteered the statement that Mr. Birch was a good man, who had been kind to him, and that what he did was by order of his Chief, whom he was bound to obey. The responsibility of the individual for his own actions was a doctrine that was strange to him, and he learnt it too late to profit by it.

In December 1876, the Maharaja Lela, the Dàtoh Sagor, Pandak Indut, and four others were arraigned before the Raja Muda Jusuf and Raja Alang Husein, and charged with murdering Mr. Birch and the others at Pàsir Sàlak on the 2nd November 1875.

They were prosecuted by Colonel Dunlop, R.A., and myself, on behalf of the Government, and defended by an able and experienced member of the Singapore Bar. After a trial which lasted eight days, they were severally found guilty and condemned to death, but the extreme penalty was exacted only in the cases of the three first named.

Sultan Abdullah, and other Chiefs whose complicity in the assassination was established by the fullest evidence, were banished from the State, and a like sentence was passed upon the ex-Sultan Ismail and some of his adherents.

In Mr. Birch the British Government lost one of its most courageous, able, and zealous officers, but, by the action which his death made necessary, the State of Perak gained in twelve months what ten years of "advice" could hardly have accomplished. That was not all, for the events of those twelve months, when they came to be fully known, threw a light on the inner life of the Malay and his peculiar characteristics, that was in the nature of a revelation.   It is all too soon to forget the lesson or disregard its teachings.

# XX

# A PERSONAL INCIDENT

Haud multum abfuit quin interfi-
ceretur

HORACE

*From* CAPTAIN SPEEDY, *Queen's Commissioner,
Larut, to* H.E. SIR WILLIAM JERVOIS,
*Governor of the Straits.*

[Extract :] LARUT, *November 9th,* 1875.

"IN the second report, that of 7th instant, Sergeant
Din states that he was told by one Kulup
Riau that Mr. Swettenham had been murdered by
the Raja Lela at Pâsir Sâlak on the 5th instant. I
regret to state that I have every reason to believe
that the report is but too true. My inspector, Din
Mahomed, reached Kuala Kangsar (where I sent
him with a party of men immediately on hearing of
Mr. Birch's death, to warn and guard Mr. Swettenham) at 2 P.M. on 4th instant, but, on his arrival,

he found that Mr. Swettenham had unfortunately left, to return by the river a few hours previously; owing to the rapidity of the current, the boats should have reached Pâsir Sâlak by the following day. I have sent detectives, both Chinese and Malay, to inquire into the matter, and to obtain, if possible, the remains of these unfortunate officers."

I came across the above passage in a Blue Book, and I will explain why Captain Speedy had every reason to believe in the certainty of my death, and how it was that my remains were not to be collected just then.

In the preceding sketch I mentioned that I left Bandar Bharu at noon on the 28th October with two boats, and intended, if it were possible, to meet Mr. Birch at Pâsir Sâlak about the 3rd November.

Besides the Malay boatmen, I had with me a very celebrated Selangor chief named Raja Mahmud, a man whose whole life had been passed in jungle warfare, and as he had come through it scathless he was regarded by Malays as invulnerable and re-spected accordingly. His latest exploit had been to take command of a body of Malays in an engagement with Her Majesty's troops in a neighbouring State (Sungei Ujong), and as I had subsequently persuaded him to go to Singapore and give himself up to the Governor, he had attached himself to me and thoroughly enjoyed the possibility of trouble in Perak.

Then I had a Manila boatman, one of the best coxswains on the river, a marvellous dancer of hornpipes and no less courageous than Raja Mahmud himself—more so he could hardly be. Lastly, Mahmud had a couple of men devoted to himself, and I had a Chinese servant.

This being the wet season the river was high, poling difficult and progress slow, so that it was not till the morning of the 30th that we reached Blanja, the village of Sultan Ismail. As Ismail had been elected Sultan by a number of influential chiefs who declined to recognise either Jusuf or Abdullah (though both of them had far superior claims), and, as by the Pangkor Treaty and re-cognition of Abdullah, Ismail no doubt felt aggrieved, I did not expect a very friendly reception from him, nor did I suppose that I should be specially welcome as the bearer of proclamations which could not be otherwise than distasteful to him. It was only six weeks since I had been at Blanja with the Governor, and again a fortnight later I went there alone. Since then Ismail (or his advisers in his name) had summoned nearly all the principal people of the upper country, and a very large number of boats had arrived at Blanja, bringing all the chiefs and their retainers. Moreover, to increase his following the ex-Sultan had resorted to an expedient not unknown in England; certain high offices of State were vacant, and into these he inducted his own adherents—in fact, created peers, to give himself a majority in the Upper House.

I waited half the day hoping to see Ismail, but failed. They said he was asleep and meant to remain asleep a long time. That is a common form of Malay diplomacy, and, as I could not afford to delay longer, I explained the proclamations, left a number of copies and said I would call on Ismail on my way back in a few days. As a piece of news they told me a customs station had been established at Blanja, and everyone who passed would be taxed, white men or Malays. I said I should be glad to see the collector, and he was introduced, but seemed embarrassed, and assured me he was only carrying out his master's orders, so I continued my journey. If any conclusion could be drawn from the conversation and manner of the

Blanja people, disturbances (war, they called it) were imminent.

The next day I was at the Raja Muda's village, and had a long talk with him. He also was for war, but did not think the Malays would begin it. He said no good would be done in the country, till "the malcontents" had been taught a lesson. Unfortunately, as far as could be seen, all the chiefs with very few exceptions, were in that category. The people hardly count, they are passive and recognise that they live to obey their leaders.

That night I reached Kuala Kangsar, and the then important personage of the place, an old lady who lived on the hill where now the Residency stands, informed me that she had been living in daily fear of attack by the people of a neighbouring village called Kôta Lâma. The shops in Kuala Kangsar were all closed, and everyone was waiting for the bursting of the storm.

The latest excitement here was that a notoriously bad character named Raja Alang, living in a house by the path which led from Kuala Kangsar to the neighbouring district of Larut, saw a foreign Malay (a man of Patâni) walking past with his wife and two children. When the man got opposite Raja Alang's house he raised his trousers to keep them out of the mud, and as Raja Alang considered this disrespectful to him, he called to the man and told him he must pay a fine of a hundred dollars. The man was of course unable to comply with this monstrous demand, so the Raja took him, his wife and children, into the house, and said he would keep them there till the money was paid. After a couple of days, during which they were given no food, Raja Alang said he would sell the woman and children to raise the amount of the fine. Just at dawn on the following morning the Patâni man got up, took from a Malay lying near him a *kris*, and with it stabbed the owner to death. Then he struck out wildly, killing another man, a woman, his own two children, and a child of Raja Alang, while he wounded his own wife. Raja Alang hastily left the house, hurting himself considerably, for he forgot the steps in the hurry of his exit. The murderer went next door and killed two more women and then escaped. Altogether he killed nine people and wounded three. It is a detail, I mention it only as showing the state of society, and because this incident, at the time of my arrival, was, with rumours of war, dividing the interests of the people of Kuala Kangsar.

On the 1st November I read and posted the proclamations in Kuala Kangsar, and on the following day I went to see the Raja Bendahara, the third highest officer in the State. He lived across the river, and to him and a large crowd of his followers I read the proclamation, and gave the Bendahara some copies, which I asked him to have posted.

Amongst the crowd was Raja Alang, who gave me his version of the *âmok*, and denied that he had ill-treated the Patâni man. I see from the journal I kept in those days that I expressed my surprise that such things were not of daily occurrence, looking to the infamous way in which the people were treated by the Rajas, to which he replied that he had done wrong but was now *taubat* (a reformed character), that he wished to go to Mecca (the desire of all Malays who want to wipe out a bad record and rehabilitate themselves with society), and would be obliged if I would lend him a thousand dollars for the purpose !

On the 3rd November I distributed the proclamations in villages between Kuala Kangsar and Larut, and in the afternoon went with Raja Mahmud and one boat up river to Kôta Lâma. This village had then, as indeed it has still, the unenviable reputation of being the most impossible place in Perak. It was a very large village, and the people in it prided themselves on their independence; their neighbours called it impudence. A few months before Mr. Birch had visited Kôta Lâma, but the people turned out with firearms, and said that if he landed they would shoot him. He had no means of forcing a landing then, nor of compelling an apology later, and, therefore, he had not since been to the place.

I had been in Kôta Lâma a month before this; I went to see a man who had been shot through the shoulder the night before by two men who had a grudge against him, and had settled it in a truly Irish fashion. They called at his house, and while engaging him in conversation and eating his *sîreh*, had measured the distance of his sleeping mat from the walls of the house. It was a wooden building, and, like all Malay houses, the floor was raised high above the ground. That night they had got underneath it, and, having carefully calculated their host's position, they fired simultaneously and decamped. One bullet missed the victim's head by an inch or two, and the other went through the floor and the mat and penetrated his shoulder.

I now went to see this man again and found him doing badly, and advised his relatives to send him to Kuala Kangsar. Then we walked about the village, talked to the people, and in the absence of the headman I sent for his deputy. He came accompanied by four or five men all armed to the teeth, and we had a conversation wherein I think each side did its best to "bluff" the other. It so happened that we had come away without the proclamations, and I asked the headman to send to Kuala Kangsar, when I got back, and I would give the papers, that he might post them in Kôta Lâma.

He said they only acknowledged one chief in Kôta Lâma, and he was the Raja Bendahara, and they would do nothing without his orders. I told them I would ask the Bendahara to give the necessary instructions, but inquired, " What about the Sultan ? " To which they replied that he lived a long way off. They added, "We won't hinder you if you want to post the proclamations," but they did not say it in the politest fashion, and I told them the permission was unnecessary, as, if I had had the proclamations, I should have posted them. After this we had a long and comparatively friendly talk, and it was nearly dark when I left them.

Raja Mahmud stood by and said nothing, but they knew well enough who he was, and it is possible they might have acted differently had he not been there. On our way back he told me he was so amazed at the way the Kôta Lâma men talked that he felt it wiser not to join in the conversation.

Arrived at Kuala Kangsar, I found the Raja Muda Jusuf, and told him the result of my visit to Kôta Lâma. The Raja Muda's feelings towards the Kôta Lâma people were quite beyond expression, and they were very cordially reciprocated.

The next morning, the 4th November, my work being done, I started down river at 8.30 A.M. I saw the Raja Muda before I left, and, again referring to my journal, I find that he said : " No early or permanent settlement can be made without force, without making an example of some of the opposition. They are quiet now because you are here ; as soon as you go they will begin again. If you and Raja Mahmud will come, and we may use force, we can settle the matter in a fortnight."

Little as he thought it, the time for force was at hand, for some was already past ; but if his prediction was right, his estimate of the means required to settle matters was over-sanguine.

Stopping only for breakfast, my boats reached Blanja at 4 P.M. It was my intention to spend the night there, interview ex-Sultan Ismail, and continue my journey the next day.

The river at Blanja shoals rapidly towards the left bank, which is bordered by a long and wide strip of sand. The boats of those who call here are dragged as close in as possible, and while our men were engaged in doing this, and still some distance from the shore, a man called Haji Ali waded out to my boat and came on board. We had noticed the unusual number of people on the sands—not less than two or three hundred—and of boats alongside there were at least fifty, but we were hardly prepared for the news that awaited us.

This Haji Ali, a tall, well-made man in the prime of life, was the genial person of evil reputation who, with Pĕnglima Prang Sĕmaun, had already distinguished himself by murdering one of the low-country chiefs. Notwithstanding this fact the Haji was always anxious to convey the impression that he was entirely friendly to me, but I distrusted him in common with the rest of the Blanja faction.

Haji Ali seated himself in my boat and at once stated that Mr. Birch had gone to Pâsir Sâlak, that there he and sixteen of his people had been murdered by the Maharaja Lela, who had then attacked and captured Bandar Bharu, killing all the Sikhs who had not saved themselves by flight. This news was so startling that I could not believe it and said so, but the man assured me it was true, and added as a proof that the Maharaja Lela had sent Mr. Birch's own boat to Blanja to prove to Ismail the truth of his statement. Ismail, he said, had declined to receive the boat, telling the men who brought it that as the Maharaja Lela had killed Mr. Birch he had better keep his boat, and the messengers had accordingly left with it only two hours before our arrival.

At Haji Ali's first words Raja Mahmud had caught up his *kris*, and was now tightening his waist-belt and preparing for instant trouble.

The Haji completed his information by considerately telling me that the Maharaja Lela and his people had staked the river right across at Pâsir Sâlak, making it impassable for boats, that they knew I was returning, and were waiting for me, it being their belief that when once they had got rid of Mr. Birch and myself they would have no further interference from white men, as no one else knew the country. He concluded with an invitation from the ex-Sultan to go and see him on shore.

I thanked him, and to get rid of him asked him to go back and say that I was coming.

As soon as he had left the boat I held a hasty consultation with Raja Mahmud, who said it would be madness to land at Blanja, where we should be like rats in a trap, and the only course was to go on at once and at all hazards before they had time to stop us.

The idea of returning up-river was unpleasant and well nigh impossible, it was therefore discarded at once.

All the men in both my boats had heard what Haji Ali said, and as some of them did not relish the prospect of trying to run the gauntlet, I decided to leave one boat and only take those who volunteered to go. That question was very soon settled, every Perak man declined the journey ; my Manila boy took the rudder, three foreign Malays and Mahmud's two men formed the crew, and Mahmud and I were the passengers. There was my Chinese servant, he was not a man of war, and I thought he would prefer to remain where he was, for they all realised that the danger would be in staying with me. When I asked him, however, he smiled a not quite pleasant smile, and producing a long knife said he did not mean to move. It was quite clear that if it came to close quarters he would give a good account of himself.

By this time we were ready to start, but just as the men were preparing to get the boat out into the stream, Haji Ali appeared again to take us on shore. I at once told him that if his story was true I could not stop at Blanja and must go on at once. How far he had been acting before was doubtful, but his surprise now was genuine enough. He said, " It is impossible, the whole country down stream is in arms, you cannot pass, it is certain destruction." We told him that whatever it was we were going, and we pointed out to him that as the boat was moving into deep water he had not much time to get out if he wanted to return to the shore. He got out, and it was rather deep, but he stood there and shouted, " No doubt you think yourselves very fine fellows, but you will be killed all the same."

He was still standing in the same place when we had gone some distance, and as we passed outside the long line of boats the many people on shore realised that we had started again and were rapidly dropping down stream. It seemed to us that for them the unexpected had happened.

The pleasure of thinking that we had at any rate cheated the Blanja people did not last us long, and believe every man in the boat—certainly I can speak for myself—believed that he had started on a journey of which sudden death was the inevitable bourne.

The Resident, we were told, had been murdered at Pâsir Sâlak, and we could not well doubt the truth of that report. Then the people on both banks of the river for miles above and below Pâsir Sâlak were on the watch for us ; the Residency was in the hands of the Maharaja Lela's people, the Sikhs killed or fugitives in the jungle ; worst of all, the river at Pâsir Sâlak was staked from bank to bank, and if so no boat could pass that barrier.

There were two points of minor moment—first, that the Residency boats were all painted white, we had one of them, and no native-owned boat in the country was white. That fact made us so conspicuous that we did not think it worth while to lower the Union Jack we carried at the stern. Secondly, up to that time no house-boat had ever made the journey from Blanja to Pâsir Sâlak in anything like twelve hours, and we calculated, therefore, that we should reach the point of greatest danger in broad daylight, probably about 9 A.M. the next morning. Speed was our best chance, but here again we were handicapped by the fact that our men had been paddling since 8.30 A.M., they had had one meal, and now there was a night's work before them and no time to stop for cooking.

If the conditions were as they had been stated,

and as we believed them to be, nothing could save us, for with two rifles and a shot gun we could hardly hope to force the barrier unless aided by a miracle.

The river was high, the current strong, and just at dusk we reached Bota. Fastened by an island opposite the village we saw Mr. Birch's own boat, the " Dragon," and with that all doubt as to his fate was at an end. Raja Mahmud suggested that we might stop and attack the people in charge. The idea was attractive and no doubt it would have been a surprise to them, but we decided that it was unwise to waste the time and rouse the whole village. As we passed the boat we could see no one in or about it.

The night was moonless but starlit, fine and clear enough for our purpose, dark enough to conceal us when we were in the middle of the stream. But the Perak is a river where the navigable channel wanders from side to side in a way that often baffles the most skilful pilot. The height of the water lessened our difficulties, but for all that we were driven at times very close to the banks. Between 9 and 10 P.M. a thick white mist came down and enveloped the river in impenetrable fog. This was very confusing, for, while it lasted, it was

impossible to see half a boat's length in any direction. The mist lifted and fell again at intervals all
through the night, and so dense was it that at one
time we lost our way, and at last discovered by a
snag that we had got the boat completely round
and were paddling up stream!

That discovery gave us rather a bad shock, for
we calculated that we had lost half an hour of precious time, and if we could make such a mistake
once it might occur again. It was possible because
we dared not have any light, and only smoked with
the utmost precaution.

I was so tired that about half-past ten I could no
longer keep awake, and several times the wearied
boatmen dropped asleep over their paddles. We
were not at all certain of our whereabouts, but
some time after eleven o'clock we realised, by the
succession of watch-fires on the banks and the
numbers of men moving about, that we were getting
into the zone of danger. It seemed to me, dozing
and waking, that this lasted for a long time ; we
were getting callous of the people on the bank when
we found that no one seemed to observe us however
close we were forced to go.

I had told them to rouse me when we got near
to Pâsir Sâlak, for now, to our great surprise, it

seemed evident that we should reach the place hours before dawn. About 1.30 A.M. Mahmud quietly woke me, and the boatmen nerved themselves for the final effort.

We knew that to get past Pâsir Sâlak it was necessary to go right under one bank or the other, and the deepest water was on the left or Kampong Gâjah side. That we decided to take. Huge fires were blazing on the bank, and round each were grouped a number of armed men—indeed, the whole place was apparently on the *qui vive.* As noiselessly as possible, but none the less vigorously, the men plied their paddles, and we made for the deep water under the bank. Just at this moment the thick white veil of mist came down over the river, and under its sheltering cover we glided swiftly down, the light of the blazing logs, close though they were, shining vaguely through the fog, while now and then a man's figure, of seemingly gigantic proportions, loomed out from the fire-lit haze.

Every instant we expected to feel the shock of the boat against the barrier, and we had determined that when that happened we would push our boat along it till we found the usual opening closed by a floating log and guarded, as we supposed, by boats. In the darkness we meant to try and force our way through or take one of the enemy's boats on the down-stream side of the stakes.

We could hardly realise the truth when we found ourselves at the lower end of the village without having encountered any obstruction. The barrier never existed in fact—only in the imagination of Haji Ali, or, more probably, the Maharaja Lela had intended to make it, but the Malay habits of laziness and procrastination defeated his plan.

Just as I was thinking a very sincere thanksgiving, the bow of the boat suddenly ran on the shore and stuck there fast. We were so close to the bank that this happened without the slightest warning. For an instant the steersman had given the rudder a wrong turn, and we were stranded. To my dismay, I saw on the high bank, exactly over us, a large fire with eight or ten men round it. I seized the shot-gun, Mahmud had a rifle, and we knelt with fingers on trigger covering two of the figures that were distinct enough in spite of the mist, for we were hardly ten feet distant from them.

Two of our men with poles were making superhuman efforts to push off the boat, when a man on the bank called out, " Whose boat is that ? " One of our men replied, " Haji Mat Yassin's," having seen his boat at Blanja. " Where are you from ? "

was the next inquiry, and the reply was, "Blanja."
"Where are you for?" and other questions followed, but by this time the bow of the boat was off
and we were drifting stern-foremost out into the
stream and the sheltering fog. As the distance
widened and shouts came to stop, the answers
returned were derisive and misleading, for everyone felt that the real danger was past and the life
he had made up his mind to lose would not be
required of him that night after all.

It was true that we had yet to pass the Residency
at Bandar Bharu, five miles lower down, and we
had been told this was in the hands of the Maharaja
Lela, but there at least there was no barrier, and
we were confident that we had nothing more to
fear.

We passed Bandar Bharu quietly, we saw a light
on each bank and a man on watch by the light, and
we said to each other that it would be very easy to
shoot the men as they placed themselves so conveniently *en évidence*.

Ten miles lower down the river, it being then
only 3 A.M., we were suddenly hailed by a voice
threatening death and other penalties if we did not
immediately declare who we were. That was a
very welcome challenge, for I recognised the voice,

and in a few seconds we were alongside a Selangor steam-launch.

Only then we learnt that Bandar Bharu had not fallen into the hands of the enemy, and we had therefore come ten miles further than was necessary; but we congratulated ourselves on the forbearance we had shown in not shooting the sentries, and later in the morning, when we got up to the Residency, suggested that if the Sikh felt lonesome in the night watches it would perhaps be wiser for him not to stand in the full blaze of a large lamp.

The Maharaja Lela and his friends professed themselves both surprised and disappointed when they found I had arrived at Bandar Bharu, having passed Pâsir Sâlak without their knowledge. I daresay, however, that some of them were not altogether sorry that they had been spared a meeting with Raja Mahmud, for he was reckoned a mighty man of valour. In my case he was also a wise counsellor, for subsequent disclosures proved that had I landed at Blanja the intention was to immediately attack and murder me, and when we so abruptly left that place the ingenuous Haji Ali and his friend the Pĕnglima Prang Sĕmaun with a number of their men were sent after us in fast boats on a mission similar to the one they had previously undertaken and successfully carried out. As we saw nothing of them I conclude they did not exert themselves to overtake us.

During the subsequent military operations in Perak, Haji Ali fell into our hands, and, after some weeks spent on a British man-of-war, he became quite a reformed character. I occasionally see him now, but he seems depressed, and when I find him looking at me there is no anger in his face, only a great sorrow as of a man who is misunderstood by the world and who suffers without resentment.

I don't know why, but this expression is a source of unfeigned amusement to the Malays who happen to see it. It is very unfeeling of them.

# XXI

# NAKODAH ORLONG

Two things greater than all things
are,
One is Love and the other War
RUDYARD KIPLING

O N the day after my arrival at Bandar Bharu,
Captain Innes, R.E., came from Penang
accompanied by two officers and sixty men of the
First Battalion of H.M. 10th Regiment, together
with the Superintendent of the Penang Police (Hon.
H. Plunket) and twenty native constables armed
with rifles.

Captain Innes, an exceptionally able member of
his distinguished corps, was then in civil employ as
head of the Public Works Department in Penang.
When the news of Mr. Birch's murder reached that
place, the nearest British Settlement, Captain Innes
was sent with a force to take charge of the
Residency.

It is not my intention to detail the subsequent events except in so far as is necessary for a right understanding of an incident connected with the death of a man called Nakodah Orlong, a Sumatran Malay.

With the force at our disposal, which included Lieut. Abbott, R.N., his four bluejackets, and about fifty so-called Sikhs, it was determined to attack Pâsir Sâlak before the Maharaja Lela had time to collect a large following. An immediate advance was also considered advisable to prevent the number of our enemies being increased by what might look like our indecision. With Easterns, to sit still and stockade your position is probably, under such circumstances, the worst course possible.

We knew that the Maharaja Lela was throwing up works, not only in his village, but outside of it, and to force them it was decided to take two howitzers and a rocket-tube.

The distance from Bandar Bharu to Pâsir Sâlak was five miles, every yard of it covered with vegetation of some sort, the only road a narrow path by the river-bank; moreover, Pâsir Sâlak was not on our side of the river. It was, therefore, settled that we should start at daylight the next morning, the 7th November, in boats, that we should pole up stream two miles and walk the rest, the guns being served by the bluejackets from two boats that would be kept in line with the shore party.

All that was wanted was a body of scouts to feel the way, and I undertook to find these. There were Raja Mahmud, his two followers, and the Manila boy already spoken of, but it was hard to say where any other trustworthy Malays could be got at such short notice. Late that evening, however, Nakodah Orlong, whom I knew well, came in, and when I asked him if he would join us he at once consented, and said he could bring fourteen of his own men with him. That made us twenty, and was enough for the purpose.

We were up at 4.30 A.M. on the 7th, got all the men into boats, and made a start by 7.30 A.M., not without difficulty, however, for we were hard pressed for hands to do the poling. It was only after we had started that I learnt the intention of taking guns had been abandoned, a very unfortunate change of plan as it turned out. To attack, without guns, any work defended by Malays means a certain sacrifice of life, as we found to our cost, and took care that the mistake was never repeated. The carriage of guns and rockets through the jungle means delay and hard work, but, whatever the trouble and delay, hardly any consideration will justify an attack without at least one gun.

The river journey was accomplished without incident, a landing was effected, and the party moved off. The scouts were in front, followed at an interval by half the detachment of the 10th, Captain Innes and the sailors with a rocket-tube came next, then the Sikhs and Penang Police under Mr. Plunket, and last of all the remainder of the 10th Regiment.

We began the march gaily enough, not expecting to meet with any resistance till near Pâsir Sâlak. After walking a mile or so, always close by the river-bank, we came to a large field of Indian corn. The plants were eight or ten feet high, and so thick and close that it was impossible to see more than three or four yards in any direction ; the ground between the corn-stalks was planted with hill-padi, and that was a couple of feet in height.

On entering this field we opened out to cover as large a front as possible, and, when half way through the corn, passed a gigantic fig-tree growing on the edge of the river bank. On my right was Nakodah Orlong, and to the right of him one of his men called Alang ; on my left was Raja Mahmud the Manila boy, and the rest of the scouts. We had been walking fast, and of the rest of the force we could see and hear nothing.

We were talking and laughing (being still a long way from Pâsir Sâlak) when suddenly we came to the end of the cover, for the last few feet of the corn had been cut down. At this moment Nakodah Orlong said, " There they are," and the words were hardly out of his mouth when we were greeted by a volley from the enemy concealed behind a stockade not a dozen yards in front of us.

Nakodah Orlong fell without uttering another sound, and, the enemy maintaining a brisk fire, our position was so uncomfortable that my own inclination was unhesitatingly to get out of the way. Probably my intention was apparent, for Raja Mahmud said, "Stand fast and shoot." I was obliged to him and followed his advice, but as the Manila boy and I were the only possessors of shooting-weapons, and the enemy were hidden behind a rampart of logs and banana-stems, while we had no shelter whatever, our continued exis- tence was due simply to their want of skill.

The absurdity of the situation was apparent, and its unpleasantness was heightened by the opening of a brisk fusilade in our rear. That decided us and we stepped back under cover, and then moved to the sheltering trunk of the fig-tree. Arrived there we found that besides Nakodah Orlong (about whose fate there was no doubt, for he fell within a yard of me), Alang was the only one missing. He was the last man on the right, and, as no one had seen him, we concluded that he also had been killed. It was at once proposed that we should go back and secure the bodies, but our own people keeping up a merciless discharge in rear, and the enemy doing their best in front, we were between two fires, and thought it best to try and stop our friends at any rate from shooting us.

We shouted, but that, of course, was no use, no one could either see or hear us, and it was some minutes before we were able to let Captain Innes know of our position. In that time we realised that even a large tree offers poor shelter from a cross fire. It did not, however, take us long to decide that the side towards the enemy was the safest.

That was only the beginning of misunderstanding ; twice again during the day we were placed in the same uncomfortable position, and a man kneeling behind me was shot in the *back* of his thigh. Once also the Sikhs made a determined attack on the men with me as we were trying to outflank the Malays, and in spite of our shouts only desisted when almost within touch of us. It is true, of course, that the cover was so dense they could not see us until the last moment. They were so dispirited by this waste of effort, that they incontinently left the place and went straight home in spite of all Plunket's attempts to stop them. That was in no sense his fault, for they were not his men, and he had never seen them before the previous evening. The Penang police had retired *en masse* at an even earlier hour, and explained afterwards, with much force, that it was not for this kind of work that they had engaged.

The enemy's stockade was a long rampart impenetrable to bullets; it was faced by a deep and wide ditch cut at right angles to the river, with one end on the bank and the other in high jungle. The work was backed by a thick plantation of bananas, affording perfect cover, and those defending it were commanded by the Maharaja Lela in person, and his father-in-law Pandak Indut, foremost of Mr. Birch's murderers.

I am not now concerned with the details of the attack, it is sufficient to say that it did not take long to prove how serious a mistake had been made in leaving the howitzers behind. The rockets, an old pattern, were ineffective, and as they all went over the top of

the stockade were greeted by the jeers of the enemy.
We were close enough to hear even what they said
in the intervals between the firing. Experience is
usually costly, and what we learnt on the 7th en-
abled us, a week later, to carry this and a succession
of other stockades without the loss of a man.

About 1 P.M. (our force being then reduced to the
officers, the men of the 10th, bluejackets, and Malay
scouts) Captain Innes gave the order to charge the
stockade. That was done, but without guns to clear
the way it was a hopeless task. We could not get
across the ditch in the face of an unseen, protected
enemy, while we were entirely at their mercy. We
had to retire with the loss of Captain Innes killed,
both the officers of the 10th (Lieutenants Booth and
Elliott) severely wounded, and other casualties. If
men with weapons of precision and the knowledge
to handle them had held the work, none of our
party ought to have escaped. But with Malays you
can take liberties ; their weapons take some time to
load, but they are deadly enough at a few yards
distance if the men who hold them would not fire at
the tree-tops. The Malay's idea is to loose off his
piece as often as he can, it makes a noise and that
puts heart into the man who fires, fear into the enemy.

Though we had gained nothing by rushing the

place, the enemy did not like that style of attack and retired, only we did not know it then. We were engaged in counting the cost, picking up the wounded and organising an orderly retreat, for it was late, we had some miles to go, and we expected the Malays would leave their shelter and come after us. Personally I did not know Captain Innes had been killed, I was in the centre and he was on the extreme right. My party was hampered by having to carry a wounded man, and when we got back to the middle of the field where Abbott and Plunket were waiting, Innes and the others had already been taken away. We had no surgeon, no stretchers, and the return journey was one that is not pleasant to recall.

We reached our boats at 3 P.M., and the Residency a quarter of an hour later.

For some time I was very busy trying to attend to the wounded, but then my Malay friends asked me for a boat, as they said they must go and fetch Nakodah Orlong's body, and see what had become of Alang. A British soldier was also missing. I gave the boat and they started.

About 8 P.M. they returned with Alang and the body of his chief; they had met the lad swimming down the river with his master's body.

When Nakodah Orlong fell, and the rest of us got away behind the great tree, this boy stayed by the dead man, and as he was right in the line of the thickest cross-fire, Alang pulled the body as close to the bank as he could, and there remained from morning till evening, making no sign, but simply declining to abandon the corpse. A man even came out from the stockade and attacked him with a *kris*, wounding him on the hand, but Alang beat him off. After the final charge, when our people passed close by him, it was he who saw the Malays retire, and he allowed us all to go away and leave him without giving any indication of his whereabouts.

Then, the coast being clear, unable to carry the body so great a distance, he dragged it into the river and was swimming down stream with it when the boat met him.

I went down to the boat to see Nakodah Orlong ; he looked just as I had seen him last, except that his hair and clothes were drenched with water and there was a great hole in the centre of his forehead, marking, no doubt, the track of an iron bullet from a swivel-gun. Of that, however, he could never have been conscious, nor yet of the devotion of the man whose life had been in extremest peril throughout a long day to guard his chief's dead body, without thought of gain or praise, only determined that none but loving hands should be laid upon the voiceless, pulseless clay he once called master.

Given a glorious sunny day and a good cause, the idea of ending existence suddenly and painlessly in the pride of life and in face of the foe has its attractions, and robs the inevitable of its sting.

But who can hope that after his death there will be one other being whose love is great enough to offer his own life a willing sacrifice to guard the thing that was to-day a friend and to-morrow will be corruption?

# XXII

# EVENING

Phœbus loosens all his golden hair
Right down the sky
                      Eric Mackay

THE tale of these little lives is told. If I have failed to bring you close to the Malay, so that you could see into his heart, understand something of his life, and perhaps even sympathise with the motives that will lead him to acts of high courage and self-sacrifice, then the fault is mine.

The glory of the Eastern morning, the freshness and the fragrance of the forest, the sultry heat of these plains and slopes of eternal green on which the moisture-charged clouds unceasingly pour fatness—these are the home of the Malay, the background against which he stands.

Come, we have done with it all ; let us leave the plain, seething in the heat of early afternoon, and ride up this mountain path, through all the wealth and the magnificence of tropical jungle, and look down on the land for the last time.

Our callous eyes—surfeited with years of gazing on brilliant colours, great stretches of sea and forest, huge trees, a bewildering luxury of foliage, beasts measured by the elephant and rhinoceros, birds by the argus pheasant and the peacock—are blind to the infinite beauty of our surroundings. This path, by which we slowly rise to cooler altitudes and a new flora, would excite in the stranger feelings of wonder and rapturous delight.

The road itself is cut through soil of a deep shade of *terra cotta*, the colour all the more vivid by reason of the hues of green by which it is environed. The sunlight strikes in rays of brilliant light across this path, falling on red soil, granite boulder and massive tree-trunk, intensifying colour and deepening shadow. Here and there are seen glimpses of the plains below, the distant sea, the peaks and valleys of other hill ranges, and the ear constantly catches the delightful sound of falling water, the voices of numerous streams dashing down the steep mountain sides in cascades of sparkling foam.

The path twists and winds, often by sharp zig-zags, up the face of the hill, across a narrow saddle and then by an even steeper ascent, till at last we gain the summit of the mountain.

Stand here. The limit of vision is wide ; you will scarce find a grander spectacle in this Peninsula. We are nearly 5,000 feet above the sea, and from north to south the eye travels over a distance not far short of two hundred miles. Eastward, those distant hills are fully a hundred miles away, and soon on the western horizon the sun will meet the sea in a blaze of glory, as though kindling at the touch of loving arms long waiting for his coming.

That faint blue peak in the north, hazy and indistinct, is Gûnong Jerai in Kedah, and the island to the westward, which smiles through a golden veil, is Penang. A grey streak of water shot with gleams of sunlight divides it from the mainland, and the forty miles of country thence to the foot of this hill, and far south again to those blue islets off the Dinding coast, lie flat and fertile, a feast for the eyes. Vivid green patches mark thousands of acres of sugar-cane and rice-field, but the general effect is an unbroken expanse of dark jungle, mostly mangrove, for all this land from hill-base to sea-shore is of comparatively recent formation, the erosion from the hills carried down seawards and covered with a wealth of foliage ever renewed by the excessive heat and excessive moisture of this forcing tropical climate. No rocks, no bare hills, no arid plains, everything covered with vegetation: new graves look old in a month, the buildings of a year, for all their seeming, might have stood for half a century.

Only at our feet does the hand of man make any mark on the landscape. There, amid trees and gardens, nestle the red roofs of Taiping. You might cover the place with a tablecloth for all its many inhabitants, its long wide streets, open spaces, and public buildings.

And those pools of water all around the town, what are those?

They are abandoned tin-mines, alluvial workings from which the ore has been removed, and water mercifully covers, in part, this desolation of gaping holes and upturned sand.

The shore, due west and distant some twenty miles from the foot of the range on which we stand, is deeply indented by three great bays. They are the mouths of three rivers, short, shallow and insignificant in themselves; it is difficult to understand why they should make such an imposing entry on the sea. A mile or two inland from the coast the eye is caught by twenty little lakes, on which the sun loves to linger, burnishing them to gold when the setting in which these jewels lie has turned to purple. They are fragments of estuaries, deep waveless lagoons winding through the mangroves, and showing to the distant spectator only broken reaches, glimpses of bay and headland.

The shore-line is a ribbon of glistening light, bordering the wide expanse of forest trees, whose roots stand deep in water when the tide is high. The mangrove cannot live beyond the reach of the brine from which it seems to draw the sap of life, and these mud flats, in their gradual accretion, are as yet scarcely above the level of the sea.

Turning to the north-east, a deep valley lies beneath us, the source of a long river, the Kurau. Miles and miles beyond rise range after range of lofty mountains, Biong and Inas and Bintang, running into the heart of the Peninsula. Further eastward is the country near the sources of the Perak River, and across the narrow valley, through which its upper waters dance in a succession of rapids, may be discerned peaks of the main range which look down on the China Sea.

Now we are facing the south-east and the valley of the Perak River. The ridge on which we stand divides it from the Province of Larut, and surely there are few fairer sights in the East than this same valley through which the river, plainly visible twenty miles away, winds in a silver streak. On the right stands Gunong Bubu, the isolated mass terminating in a needle-like point nearly 6000 feet high. The spurs of this mountain spread out in every direction, north to the Pass from Larut into the Perak Valley, east to the Perak River, and southwards nearly to the coast. In the south-east, across the Perak River, rise five or six ranges of hills of ever-increasing height. Over the first range can be seen the valley of the Kinta, with its many fantastic limestone cliffs standing clearly out ; then follow Chabang, Korbu, and finally the mountains dividing Perak from Pahang. Those hills fading out of sight in the far-away south are near the borders of Perak and Selangor.

As we turn our faces back to the setting sun, the great disc, now grown a deep crimson, is sinking through a bank of clouds into a sea of flame. The waters beyond the influence of the sun's light are a brilliant sapphire, a reflection of the sky above. There is only one long, low bank of cloud, and that is on the horizon.

A moment later and the sun itself has gone, but from the spot where it disappeared is radiating a lurid glow which kindles the clouds into fire and shoots rays of gold over Penang in the north and the Dinding Islands in the south, seventy miles apart. This golden light spreads for a space upward through the bank of clouds, till, paling into a belt of grey that again deepens into blue, and ever gaining in intensity, it rises to the zenith and fills the empyrean.

Meanwhile the darkness which seemed to be settling over the distant eastern ranges is gradually suffused with soft tints of *rose dorée*, transfiguring peak after peak and clearly defining every ridge and valley. This aftermath of day, wherein the sun returns to kiss the hills with one last lingering caress, fills the whole atmosphere with a rosy effulgence, then fades reluctantly away. 'Twixt western sea and eastern hill lies that great sea-indented plain over which night settles slowly but surely, while still the sky and hills are vivid with colour. But even the plain assumes its night garb with no less grace and beauty. A faint mist has risen from swamp and river, and, spreading itself over the land, takes soft hues of opal and heliotrope deepening into purple, while only the pools and river-reaches shine out, like scraps of mirror stealing borrowed glory from the sky.

Soon this light wanes ; purple turns to grey, the

colours fade from sky and sea, only the shore-line keeps its sheen. Then this too dies, and great white clouds, coming from out the mines and marshes·like a troop of giant spectres risen in their grave-clothes, stalk slowly round the foothills of the mountain, through the Pass into the valley of the Perak River.

Here, at this elevation, the night is not quite yet.

Close around us still the jungle, but the trees are dwarfed, the boughs are covered with moss and lichen, orchids and ferns flourish in the forks, gorgeously blossomed creepers twine round the branches and hang from tree to tree. The air is full of the scent of the magnolia, the moss-carpeted ground is gay with a myriad flowers, some brilliantly plumaged songless birds flit silently between the trees, and a great bat sails aimlessly across the waning light. The shrill scream of the cicada is but faintly heard far down the height, and night comes, like a closing hand grasping in resistless darkness all things visible. The only sound to break the silence is the fitful and plaintive croak of a wood-frog.

If night treads closely on the heels of day, there is no need for regret. The darkness is but for a moment, and over the eastern peaks spreads a silvery sheen, herald of that great orb of splendour which, rising rapidly, clears the mountain and sheds a flood of wonderful, indescribable, mellow radiance over forest, plain, and sea, softening what is crude, pointing with brilliance the most striking features, and casting into a fathomless shadow the dark valleys of the western slopes. There is nothing cold about this Eastern moon. Seen, half-risen, against the dark foliage of the mountain, it glitters like molten silver, dazzling the eyes, and as it soars serenely upward seems the very perfection of beauty, light, and purity.

Strange that the delight and glory of mankind since ever the earth was peopled, the emblem of unattainable longing, should be only a gigantic cinder.

Printed by BALLANTYNE, HANSON & Co.
London & Edinburgh